FLUID

Out of Darkness Comes Light

Tiffany Maxwell & Savannah Jenkins

Glover Lane Press
Publishers Since January 2000
www.gloverlanepress.webs.com

FLUID: Out of Darkness Comes Light
Copyright Owned by Noble Trinity Publishing.
www.tiffanyandsavannah.com,
www.tashiaasanti.com www.skyearthfire.com
Bookings through www.nobletrinitymusiclabel.com

Cover Design by Azaan Kamau
Author images provided by Ifalade Ta'Shia Asanti

Published by Glover Lane Press
ISBN-13: 978-0615914909
ISBN-10: 061591490X

The Mission of Glover Lane Press is to Uplift, Empower, Elevate the Masses and Provide American Jobs. Every book published by Glover Lane Press and its many imprints, is printed and manufactured in the United States of America, ensuring and maintaining American employment.

"Reality doesn't impress me. I only believe in intoxication, in ecstasy, and when ordinary life shackles me, I escape, one way or another. No more walls." Anais Nin

Fluid is a collection of fiction stories celebrating the birth of a new movement—a movement honoring the sacredness and power of a woman's desires and the beauty and strength of masculine energy.

Each story is a testimony of bravery and courage. To speak of our desires, the wants and needs we rarely, if ever, speak of…this is healing in and of itself.

If you are a woman reading this book, we ask that while you read, you give yourself the gift of being every bit of who you are, without judgment, fear, shame or restraint.

If you are a man partaking in these delectable pages, may you fully indulge in the pleasure of these words, taking from them all you seek to know and understand of you & the women in your lives.

To our fans, we invite you to discover and rediscover your passion on these pages. Fluid knows no limits of age, gender, race or culture. Fluid becomes as the reader unveils her. Join us as we journey to the place where life becomes FLUID….let your wings open, become whole and take flight. But remember, as you fly--DO HARM TO NONE…

May you know fluidity in its most sacred form...YOU.

With Love, Tiffany and Savannah

<u>Dedications</u>-Tiffany

Fluid is dedicated to my life partner, Pepper. For flowing with me, for blessing me with your love, passion and support always. Fluid is because we are...I love you eternally my sweetheart.

To my family, friends and students—know always that you are worthy of your desires. Celebrate every one!

To our readers-Give yourself the gift of being Fluid at least once a day, two if you are bold...

To Azaan Kamau—thank you for seeing the vision of Fluid and signing on to be the channel through which She would come to earth. The journey continues.

To Savannah-Thanks for being my muse, for being my sistah, for turning my eyes to my own womb for healing. Maferefun Oya for her work in making and keeping love strong....

Dedications-Savannah

To Bumble, it was because of your questioning my desire to want to share these words with the world, I moved on with it, said yes and never second guessed the power in my YONI. Thank you for your support, love, encouragement and for believing that I can do all things. Daisy

To my mother Bessie, thank you for always having my back and for your unwavering support for everything that I do, every dream, ever want and every desire. Thank you for living vicariously through me! It's been a blast hasn't it!

To my son's thank you for always being my source of inspiration. You are my everything! AN-ZAY-STONE I love you!

To my family and friends for being the rock that grounds me and for always welcoming my new ideas and dreams with open arms, you are always there cheering me on and I am filled with gratitude.

To my twin Tiffany who appeared on my path as I flapped my wings heavenly searching for my divine destiny. It was your high vibration that moved me swiftly into the right direction so that I could see clearly my new journey. Thank you for pushing me to write these sexy words. May our syconized motion always come from our vibrant, powerful root and heart chakra engraved with love. And when we are old and gray may we always dance and rejoice in the power of the yoni! LOVE! Savannah

To our readers, let there never be a day that you go unsatisfied. Let your fantasies and wants be like a hobby to you. enjoy it and do it as much as you can. Release Rejuvenate and Revitalize! You can say yes to pleasure anytime you want, it is your call. You own it!

You are the reason we are FLUID....

Testimonies

Hurricane-Tiffany Maxwell 12

The Sleepover-Tiffany Maxwell.. 50

The Dark Angel By Ifalade Ta'Shia Asanti.................................... 134

Swan-Tiffany Maxwell-Ifalade TaShia Asanti 157

Bound-Savannah Jenkins.. 229

Enslaved-Savannah Jenkins... 235

Reminisce-Savannah Jenkins.. 244

Freedom by Savannah Jenkins.. 250

Flight #69-By Savannah Jenkins 254

About the Authors.. 259

TIFFANY
MAXWELL

Fluid Wisdom

Love is not ordinary. Every love is an original blueprint created by the individuals expressing it. Love cannot be contained by human emotions such as fear and possessiveness. Love in its most pure form roams free, even between those who are committed to one another. When love allows each person to be their fullest self, it continues to grow, expand and evolve throughout its history...

Hurricane-Tiffany Maxwell

Anais needed a fix. Running was the drug she chose to get high. The rhythm of her feet hitting the pavement. The chill of the crisp air on her face. Together it made all that was unsure as clear as the sun rising in the sky.

Today the sky was gloomy and mysterious. Ominous clouds loomed like they were harboring messages. Anais was tempted to stay indoors where it was warm and dry. But true runners never let a little bit of weather keep them from putting in the time.

She snatched a pair of purple runners from the closet, slid her full hips into bright yellow leggings and wiggled into a purple sweatshirt. She strapped on a small green backpack, put her hair in a simple bun and started the timer.

She was two miles and some change into her run when the first cloud broke. Its fluid poured onto the streets drenching everything it touched. When her runners were too soaked to keep going, she dashed into the lobby of *Chateau Mystique*, a chic new hotel in the heart of downtown Palm Springs.

When she exited the ladies room a handsome man and his lovely companion were sitting by the fireplace next to the bar sipping Expresso. The woman had legs as long as the Nile and breasts that could make a cold room warm. Her flawless skin was the color of caramel. Her hair was a buttery blonde.

The long-legged woman's date was GQ'd down with a brown *Hugo Boss* suit, mustard shirt and amber tie. Anais got a whiff of his woody aftershave. His picture-perfect smile had the power to wake the dead.

Anais slid her jacket off her shoulders and let the heat from the crackling flames warm her body and dry her soggy clothes. When she turned toward the crackling fire she caught Mr. Handsome taking in her voluptuous curves.

"Rain chased you down, huh?" He asked, mildly flirting but keeping it respectful enough not to piss off his blonde bombshell.

"Yeah, guess it did. Was hoping to get in at least five but had to throw the towel in two miles early."

"I'd do good to get in two on those inclines. You must run these hills a lot."

His girlfriend's radar tuned in to their friendly chatter.

The man was digging for information. Wanted to know if she was a local or just passing through town. Curiosity got the best of her. She decided to play the mouse to his cat for a little while.

"I know these roads pretty good. But today's different. The wet pavement makes it hard to focus. Slippery and dangerous out there."

"Well, I applaud your commitment. Hey—excuse my manners. I'm Roderick Michael Bowen and this is Winona Lenway, one of the models for my show."

14

"Nice to meet you Roderick Michael Bowen. You too Winona. Anais Wilson here. Freelance software consultant."

Roderick held on a tad too long when he and Anais shook hands. His model friend gave a polite nod in her direction which Anais knew was code for *back off bitch, he's taken.*

"Can I get you a hot coffee, tea or something to help you warm up?"

"I'm fine. Fire's doing its job on my clothes and it looks like the rain is slowing down. Gonna try to finish the last few miles of my run. Thanks for the offer though."

She slid a business card from her backpack. "If your company's ever in the market for software that'll make your systems run like clockwork, give me a call."

Roderick flipped a gold-emblazoned business card out of a diamond encrusted case.

"And if you ever want to immortalize that fabulous body in a magazine or on a runway, you give me a call."

"You're sweet but I'm way too old to start a modeling career."

"There's a whole lot more to modeling than runways."

His model friend cleared her throat to let him know she'd had enough.

"You ready, Winona?"

"Yes. Getting hungrier by the minute."

"Steak or fish?"

"Fish." Winona answered nodding at Anais.

"Anais, you have a good evening." Roderick said, taking Winona's elbow.

As they moved by her Anais noticed his hands. They were a work of art. His hands took her eyes downtown to his feet. She was done after that. Cooked like a goose.

She pulled her damp sweatshirt over her head and dropped a seed in the garden of brewing lust.

"Hey, there's a great seafood restaurant on North Palm Canyon Blvd. It's called *Riccio's*. Place where all the locals go for good fish."

His eyes lit up the way lightning flashes when it stretches across the sky. "Sounds good. You...you want to join us?"

"Not exactly dressed for dinner."

"If you change your mind, come on down. We're slow eaters."

Slow eaters.

She wondered if Roderick's words were sexual innuendos.

Anais waved her goodbyes at the mysterious Roderick Michael Bowen and his blonde bombshell before trotting down the rain washed streets.

17

She made it home forty five minutes later. Started yanking off her sweaty clothes as she walked in the door. She was in her birthday suit by the time she made it to the bathroom.

She checked her watch. Felt proud she'd broken her best two mile time. She decided that was a good enough reason to celebrate. She popped the cork on a bottle of Riesling, turned on the bubbles in the Jacuzzi and sunk down into the soothing steam.

As she sipped, she thought about Roderick Michael Bowen. His alluring scent and immaculate body. That hypnotic smile and those long feet.

Half-hour later she was tipsy, on the edges of being downright drunk. Her hand drifted to her kitty. When her fingers connected with the pearl, she realized she was swollen. She parted her lower lips and exposed the sweet flesh inside.

She massaged herself softly, let the pleasure melt over her in ripples. She turned over on her stomach and let the Jacuzzi jets rain over that special spot.

She imagined Roderick's hands caressing her body, squeezing her nipples, making their way down her stomach to her kitten. She felt him sliding in one finger, then two, while licking and sucking the diamond between her legs.

She fantasized sliding her hand down his firm stomach to that rock in his pants. Feeling its soft ridges in the palm of her hand. Taking it out, sliding her mouth up and down it until he couldn't take anymore.

She threw her head back and waited for the explosion she needed to get the monkey off her back. It came and went so fast that the pleasure was diminished. When it was over—when the throbbing had stopped, she was clear it was barely enough to carry her through the night.

She knew what the kitty needed to make it purr.

She stepped out of the tub, wrapped a thick towel around her waist, went to her bedroom, opened the drawer and pulled out the *Rabbit*.

She clicked on the power and waited for him to come to life. All she got was a low hum. Batteries were darn near gone. She rambled through a couple of drawers but knew she was SOL by the time she got to the third drawer. Zelch. Nada.

"Damn. What's a girl gonna do?"

She sat on the edge of the bed, moisturized her toned body with a layer of almond oil. She went to the closet, flipped through a few of her favs, settled on a form-fitting black lycra dress. She slid her nines into a pair a black stilettos, dabbed frankincense perfumed oil on her pulse points and headed for the door.

Anais knew exactly where she was going but pretended she didn't. Three green and one red light later, she was sitting in the parking lot of *Riccio's* questioning her sanity.

20

"Fuck it."

She got out of the car and walked toward the entrance of the restaurant. Half way there, she turned around and walked back toward her car. As she walked, she tried to talk herself out of going inside.

"You don't know these people. They might be crazy. Go home while you still can."

She stood at the car door, keys in hand.

"You need to learn how to enjoy life." She parroted the words that Zora, her BFF, had spoken in her ear during their Girlfriend's Retreat in Las Vegas the month before.

"Not at the expense of my safety, Miss Zora." Anais said, convinced she'd just had an epiphany.

She heard someone walking up behind her. She smelled him before she saw him.

"Anais Wilson. We meet again. Saw you from the window. You wanna come in and have a glass of wine?"

It was Roderick Michael Bowen and all his fineness. He'd seen her walking back and forth like a lunatic and came out to seal the deal with his bewitching smile.

"I...I don't want to intrude on you and Winona's date."

"She works for me. We aren't...we're not a couple. And we're not alone. We hooked up with a few of my team members. Why don't you come on in and join us? It'll be fun. I promise."

Knowing there was a group inside made her feel at ease when Roderick offered her his elbow and escorted her into the restaurant.

When they got to the table he pulled up a chair next to him. She sat close enough to inhale his sweet, minty breath and musky body. She found herself thinking about sitting in his lap, putting her lips on that trumpet in his pants and....

"Evelyn, Richard, Salena, meet Anais Wilson. She's a Software Consultant. And a runner."

They nodded their hellos as Roderick went around the table and introduced them.

Salena, the Latin sister, was a pop singer. Anais admired her beautiful dark skin. She clearly had some island DNA. Maybe Puerto Rico or Cuba in her ancestral line. She reminded Anais of Joseline from that *Love & Hip Hop in Atlanta* reality show.

The consummate money man, Richard was suited and booted, wearing the finest Italian threads a working stiff could afford. He looked like a young Brad Pitt with his tousled brown hair and thick eyebrows.

Evelyn was a southern girl. Her daylight gig was on the *Food Network* as a gourmet chef. She modeled for RMB Fashion part time. Her infectious drawl, that apple bottom butt she was toting—Anais pegged her for ATL, Alabama or Kentucky born.

23

"And you met Winona earlier."

"Yes. Hello, again, Winona."

Winona nodded her perfunctory you-ain't-nobody-but-hello nod.

Richard spoke first. "So they actually have Black folks in Palm Springs?"

"Absolutely. And most of us are upscale. A few of us are wealthy. Most of the brothers come down here to hide out with their mistresses. Kind of lonely for a single girl."

Roderick took the lead in the conversation.

"And you? What brought you to this dessert oasis?"

"Cheap real estate and no traffic. Thought I could flip a few properties and relocate to one of the more quiet burbs in L.A. Then I met a guy who'd just masterminded some groundbreaking software. He talked me into heading up his marketing team. Offered me a ridiculous amount of money, a fresh-off-the-lot beamer and a condo on Palm

Canyon with a swimming pool and a Jacuzzi. Who could turn down a deal like that?"

Everybody at the table nodded their agreement.

"Anais, we know you just got here but we're headed back to my hotel suite to watch Winona's audition for *American Top Model*, sip on some Yack and network. Richard's got some stock I'm interested in and Salena has a screenplay she wants to tell us about. Care to join us?"

"I'm a little hungry. I might stop by later."

"Why don't you order room service from my suite?"

"It's so expensive. I'm trying to stay on a budget so when I leave this desert I can live and travel where ever I want."

"Ladies don't pay for their meals when they're in the company of real men."

Her smile told him she was impressed.

She downed the last of her wine.

"Guess I'm in then."

"Great. Let me take care of the check and we're out."

He signaled the waiter.

Anais talked to cover up her nervousness.

"This wine is excellent. What's the vintage?"

His answer would tell her everything she needed and wanted to know about him.

"1973 Peter Michael. Sommelier recommended it. He said they fly it in from up north. First time I had it was at the Fairmont in Kona. Peter and I have been the best of friends ever since."

Right answer Anais thought to herself.

Winona rode with Richard and the other girls back to the hotel. Anais stayed behind and waited while Roderick paid the check. When he was done, Roderick walked Anais to her car. She had a nice buzz from the wine she drank at home and the wine she had after she got to the restaurant. If she didn't eat, it wouldn't be long before she needed a nap or worse, a toilet.

A few feet from her vehicle, Anais stepped on a rock and almost went down. If she hadn't been intoxicated she would've been watching where she was walking. Roderick grabbed her around the waist and pulled her to him to keep her from falling.

While she regained her balance, her ass was pressed into his pelvis region for two long minutes. Two minutes was long enough for her to know that the man was *blessed.*

"You alright? I think you need to let me drive. You're...really relaxed. That's a good thing if you're at home but not if you're about to get behind the wheel."

"I'm...fine. I just live up the street. I'll...I'll just go on home."

She didn't know him well enough to leave her car behind. Especially to go to a hotel with four strangers.

"Look, I just dropped a hundred G in this one-horse town. I'm a successful business man with a major public presence. Saying that to say, you're safe. If you don't believe

27

I'm who I say I am, Google me right now. I just don't want you to hurt yourself or somebody else driving under the influence."

"Well..."

"Look, I'll take you to the hotel and get you some coffee and food. You and Winona can go pick up your car after you mellow out."

She did the math in her head.

She lived two miles from the restaurant and five miles from the hotel. If she had to walk home she could. She'd also make sure the front desk staff of the hotel saw her go in with him.

"It's cool. You're right. Friends don't let friends drive drunk."

His pearl colored Maserati was parked three cars down.

"Nice ride." She told him as he opened the door and let her in.

When he slid into the driver's seat he said, "Nice business investment."

"New age business psychology. If you can't write it off, you shouldn't buy it."

"Exactly. So what'd you do before you got into the software business?"

"Stripper." She joked as he pulled out and onto the road.

"Sense of humor. Cute. What'd you really do?"

"Real estate. Made my capital flipping houses. Flipped dang near a hundred of those bad boys."

"Impressive but I'd still like to see you on the pole."

"I see I'm not the only one with jokes."

"Let me cut to the chase. I'm interested in you."

"Interested in fucking me or knowing me?"

"Frankly, both."

"We just might be able to arrange that."

Roderick smiled and said, "I love a direct woman. Find it sexy as hell."

"And I dig a straight up, no chaser, man."

They pulled up to the hotel, valeted the vehicle and took the elevator up the penthouse. When they opened the door to the penthouse, Anais damn near lost her breath.

The scene inside that room was like a hurricane. It swept you up into it, made you do what it wanted, defied your body's natural inclination to turn away and run.

Salena's wrists and ankles were bound to the desk chair. Evelyn was on the floor between her legs sucking her. Her fingers were pumping like she was looking for oil. She had Salena moaning like a banshee.

Directly behind them, Winona was on the bed on her hands and knees. Richard was behind her. His love muscle working her pussy like it was his employee. Winona stuck her ass high in the air and backed that thing up in warp speed.

Salena's eyes opened for brief moment but she was too far gone, too close to orgasming to stop. Evelyn gripped Salena's hips and slid her booty forward so she could get to her pearl a little better. That sent Salena over the top.

Roderick seemed like he was as shocked as Anais but she be couldn't sure he hadn't known what would be going down when they got there.

Almost as if he was reading her mind he said, "Okay. This isn't exactly what I had in mind."

"Are we....we gonna leave?"

"That's up to you. The penthouse is huge and it's no problem for us to go to another room."

Anais told herself to leave, to walk back down the hall to the elevator and go home. But her feet were stuck. Felt like she was standing in cement and couldn't move.

"Well, what's it gonna be?"

"As long I'm not required to participate, I'm cool. I do enjoy watching though I've never done it in person. Watched my fair share of porn in this lifetime."

Roderick moved the party inside and closed the door.

He took her to another part of the suite. They could still hear but not see the sex fest going on in the adjoining rooms. He got on the phone, ordered her some food, a pot of coffee and a light dessert.

Twenty minutes later they were scarfing, laughing and talking like old friends. Anais had almost forgotten about the orgy going on in the other room. Then it happened, the moment lovers lived for. The activity taking place just a few feet away from them became real again.

Salena was the first one to come. They knew this not because they saw it but because Roderick, Anais and everyone else in the *Chateau Mystique* heard her yell it at the top of her lungs.

"I...I...I'm coming. Oh shit! I'm fucking coming for you, Evelyn. Fuck yeah. Oh God. I'm coming for youuuuuu!"

Anais paused mid-chew to acknowledge Salena's earthshaking orgasm. It was beautiful. She could feel the pleasure deep down in her bones. This was the moment during sex that a woman became fluid. When nothing but ecstasy existed in her body, mind and soul.

Roderick was moved too. To keep his cool, he went out on the balcony, lit a cigar and took a long toke. Anais joined him with a tall, chilled glass of iced tea.

Both of them were speechless for a minute or two.

"I don't want you to get the wrong impression. I mean, I know that my people have some wild parties during fashion week but typically they do it in their own suite."

"I'm fine. I mean, I gotta admit, I was shocked when we first opened the door but I'm a big girl. Plus, my head's a lot clearer since I ate something."

"Can I ask you a question?"

33

"I may not answer but you can ask away."

"Why'd your mother name you Anais? You know who she was right?"

"Of course I do. Anais Nin wrote, *Reality doesn't impress me. I only believe in intoxication, in ecstasy, and when ordinary life shackles me, I escape, one way or another. No more walls.* She was the matriarch of sexual liberation. She believed women were Gods and deserved to be worshipped. She believed a woman should have no guilt or shame about her sexual desires. I'm impressed that you know about her."

"So….do you believe what she believed?"

"To a point. Can't say I'm as free as her but I'm pretty liberal in the area of sex. Had my share of over the top experiences. When I get married, gonna lose my freaking mind."

"Why do you have to wait until you get married? Is it religion or are you saving it for that special one?"

34

"I'm not necessarily waiting but I do wanna save a few firsts for the man I say I do to."

"Nothing wrong with that."

His next question surprised her.

"Should I assume there's no one special in your life right now?"

"I have candidates for the election but haven't selected anybody for the final race."

He chuckled. "What would you say if I told you I'd like to toss my hat in the ring?"

"I'd say I'll think about it. Gotta find out what your platform issues are."

In the next room, Winona was approaching the finish line. Winona was a screamer. Richard was banging the lining out of it. You could hear his package slapping against her thighs from the next room.

"Yes. Yes! Yessssss! Fuck me, Richard! Harder. Come on, baby. Give me that dick. I want that dick. Gotta have that diccccckkkkk. I'm coming you bastard. Oh shit…I'm coming!"

Richard was about to lose it too. He started spanking her ass, taking his balls to the wall every five seconds.

"Yeah! Take all this. Aw, fuck yeah…..There….there it is. I'm….Coming. Shittttt. I'm coming!"

Roderick looked over at Anais, picked up his bill fold and the keys to his car.

"I think I've had enough. You wanna take a ride?"

"I couldn't agree more. Let's rock."

They drove in silence, both of them still covered in the energy of the sex fest taking place in Roderick's penthouse. They ended up right where they started, *Riccio's*.

He walked her to her car for the third time that day. She put her key in the door and turned around to thank him. The next thing she knew, she was in his arms.

"Meeting you was incredibly refreshing, Anais."

"You too. Have a good evening. I…." She struggled yet again with telling him farewell.

"Yes?"

She went in her purse, took out a pen and opened his hand. She wrote something on his palm and after a slow, savory kiss on his lips, she got in her car and drove off.

Thirty-two minutes later there was a knock at her front door. She turned off the bathwater and raced to answer it.

"Of course I want to end this evening the right way." He told her before placing his thick, sexy lips on top of hers for a long passionate kiss.

When they paused to catch their breath she asked him, "What took you so long?"

"GPS had me lost. Plus I stopped to get you a present."

"A present? You really want my Electoral vote don't you."

"I aim to please."

She opened the brown paper bag his gift came in and looked inside.

"It's a bottle of the 1973 Peter Michael! How'd you find it on such short notice?"

"A man has his resources. If he's a smart man that is. Why don't you fill a couple of glasses for us while I take a quick shower. It's been a long day and I need to freshen up."

Anais paused before answering. It had been a while since a man walked around naked in her house.

"Shower's back here. I'll get you a towel."

She let him use the shower in her guest room. As soon as he got in, she made a dash for the bathtub. After cleaning every crevice and fold that might be tasted or touched, she applied a coat of rose-scented lotion and dotted her wrists and thighs with ylang-ylang oil.

When she came out he was chilling on the couch, flipping through her latest copy of *Forbes,* wearing a white wife beater and red boxers. Anais had on a long black Kimono robe with a red dragon on the back. Underneath was a sexy black thong and matching lace bra. Her hair was in a high ponytail. She let the robe trail behind her like a cape as she sashayed across the floor.

"Lei è una bella vista da vedere." He said in flawless Italian.

"Thank you. You're a beautiful sight to behold too."

"Lei parla italiano?"

"Molto poco, solo un po. Only a little."

"Sei fantastico!"

"Are you Italian, Roderick?"

"My mother was. My father is African-American."

"I'm sorry to have made you think about your mother."

"It's okay. Really. Come sit with me. Vieni qui amore mio."

She sat down next to him. Felt a little shy. She pulled the robe tight around her soft flesh. She felt an almost magnetic pull from his warm, muscular body.

He let his hand rest on her thigh. He pulled the material back a few inches to glimpse her assets.

"Mmmm, nice."

Roderick smelled like coconut and cocoa—the remnants of her Brazil Nut shower gel. She fought the urge to taste his skin, to run her hand over his soft, hairy chest and peek at the treasure down below.

Roderick wanted to be sure he wasn't overstepping her boundaries.

"Is this okay with you? Me touching you?"

"I wouldn't have given you the address if I didn't want you here. I do need to ask about your HIV status."

He went in his wallet, took out a folded piece of paper and handed it to her.

"Is that what I think it is?" She unfolded the paper. "It's less than thirty days old."

"I take one every month. Just in case I get lucky."

She got up, went to her bedroom and came back with her own folded up sheet of paper.

"Mine is six months old. But it really doesn't matter."

He knew she meant that she hadn't been with anyone to make that status change.

"It's not foolproof. We're still trusting each other's word."

"I trust you." Roderick said in husky voice that made Anais' knees weaken.

He opened her robe. Leaned over and kissed the flesh on her right thigh. His lips were hot. Felt like fire on her skin. She lit up like a string of Christmas lights.

"Before we do this, just want you to know I expect nothing beyond tonight."

He smiled and asked, "That your way of telling me you only want sex?"

"No. Just don't want you to think you owe me anything."

"What if I want to owe you?"

"It could be nice having you in my debt."

"Think I'll start paying my bill right away."

He dragged his tongue down her leg to her feet. Put her toes in his mouth and sucked.

She laughed, moaned and pushed him away.

"Ticklish huh? I'll have to remember that."

He kissed the bend of her knee, sucked on her skin a bit, moved up another inch, repeated the process again. She gasped, let the sensations move through her like wildfire.

When he got to her triangle dome, he licked around it, blew his hot breath on her center, spread her like butter and sampled her heat.

"That feels good...mmmm....don't stop."

He slid her thong to the side. Wrapped his lips around her freshly shaved mound, pulled her into his mouth, locked her pleasure between his tongue and teeth.

"Mother of God….you're amazing. You must have a Ph.D. in cunnilingus."

He sucked and stretched it with his lips. First he did it soft then he gave it to her hard. Did it like that until a lake of nectar was flowing from her.

He reveled in her response. "You're so fucking wet. What you want from me? Tell me, sweet Anais? Huh? What the baby want?"

"You know what She wants."

He sucked her some more. Turned and twisted it in his lips. Had her writhing, begging him for it like it was air.

"Please….Roderick….I need it. Give it….to me."

"You ready for the hurricane?"

"Yes, I'm ready…so ready."

He spread her legs with his knees. Let the tip of the Hurricane hang out at the entrance of her juicy folds.

She tried to ride down on it. He stopped her.

"Don't move. Let me do all the work for now."

He put the tip inside of her and pulled it out. Did that five, six, seven more times.

"Fuck you. Fuck you for torturing me like that."

He dropped down and sucked it some more. Just when she was about to come, he stopped.

"The sooner you accept that I'm running this show, the better off you'll be."

She clawed at his back. Begged him to do whatever he wanted with her body.

"Turn over on your stomach and spread 'em."

She did exactly what he told her.

He put the tip inside of her again then slid the whole nine inches in at one time.

She screamed, "Oh…God…I'm coming! Coming all over your sweet dick!"

The first vestiges of his own climax hit him. "Don't….don't come yet. Wait…"

He took it all the way out, sld it all the way in. She fought to stay still, to be obedient tc his command.

He slapped her ass on the fleshy part. Made her skin sting with the vibration of pleasure and pain combined.

"Now move that ass for me, Anais. Move it while I fuck you and play with your pussy."

He wiggled his finger back and forth over her magic button. Pumped the Hurricane in and out of her until she lost it, until *they* lost it simultaneously.

Their spirits left this earthly plane. Nothing and no one existed except the orgasms that were ripping through their bodies.

Anais had no idea who was speaking through her and as her.

"I'm fucking you fucking you fucking you coming so damn hard you son-of-a-bitch shit motherfucka! That's how you fuck me goddamnit. Oh shit…I can't stop…coming…I'm coming coming coming yes! Fuck yes cominggggg!"

Roderick uttered similar vulgarities. "This. Pussy. So. Damn. Good. Fuck. Hell yeah. This pussy is so good! So fucking good this pussy is." Roderick yelled as the come shot out of him like lightning.

After their heartbeats slowed, when Roderick's Hurricane started to diminish, they slapped hands in a mutual high five like they'd just won an Olympic gold medal.

Anais slithered off the couch, crawled across the floor to the bathroom, grabbed a towel, crawled back through the living room to the couch.

His love was running down her thighs. The Hurricane glistened with her juices.

They laid there for a while, their chests rising and falling, basking in the bliss of the phenomenal sex they'd shared. Roderick broke the silence with yet another compliment.

"Voglio sapere che la signorina Wilson. Voglio sapere che al di là di questa sera."

"You lost me on that one. Something about beyond tonight?"

"What I said Miss Wilson, was *I want to know you.* I want to know you beyond tonight."

"I think I can handle that."

He pointed toward her kitchen. "You have food in there? I need to build my strength back up. Hope you didn't think you were getting off that easy."

"I can whip us up a little something. If you promise to be good for the rest of the night."

"I'mah be good alright. I think you better look out the window at the sky."

47

"What? What you see?"

"I think there's a Hurricane brewing. His name is Roderick Michael Bowen. He's coming to visit you. He might just stay for a while."

"You better let him know that not only do I have a generator but down in my basement, there's enough food and supplies to make it until the winds die."

"What you don't know, Miss Wilson, is that this is a special hurricane. These winds don't die. Just get stronger and stronger as time goes by."

Fluid Wisdom

At the core of every love is a deep need crying out to be fed. Affection, understanding, sensual satisfaction or recognition. These are among the hundreds of needs met through the interchange of love. In loveships that are fluid, each person's needs are recognized, honored and affirmed. Even when a need cannot be met, it is at the very least, acknowledged. This way, no desire or need is ever left behind and we never, ever, do harm to none.

The Sleepover-Tiffany Maxwell

Indulgence is a fire that once ignited can only be extinguished by those who dare to dance with its intoxicating power. Her succulence draws you in, renders you helpless to her sweet, seductive charm. But do be warned, Lady Indulgence can turn on you. She'll drain the blood from your heart while wearing a coy smile on her face. Mostly she is merciful. She releases her subjects with a slap on the hand. The question of the hour remains: how far are you willing to go to eat the fruits of her sacred garden?

Kalina Santiago had done her fair share of sexploration but this—what her husband Merrill was asking her to do now—would take their vows to a whole new level.

Merrill Santiago had gone to one of those *Tantric Sex* workshops to prepare for the opening of *Destiny Awakened*, their new day spa. Merrill tried to convince her it was no big

50

deal—said he wanted to put some unique offerings on their Spa menu to give them the edge over their competitors. Kalina felt like it was just a line to get her to consider what he really wanted—a total freak in his bed at night.

She agreed to go to one class with him just to see what it was all about. She expected the teacher to be some middle-aged, flabby woman living out her sexual fantasies through her students. Instead, Mahkta Patel, head instructor and founder of *Erotic Journeys Institute* turned out to be a total Goddess...

When Kalina saw Mahkta she understood why Merrill wanted a second class. Mahkta's long, black hair danced on her shoulders as she moved her hypnotic body around the room. A native of India, Mahkta's sultry accent made her voice sound exotic and mysterious.

Merrill came out of the bathroom drying his hands. His burgundy velour sweat suit and white tank fit his toned body like a glove. His curly black hair and dark eyes made

51

Kalina's insides melt like bubble gum in the sun. Merrill joined her in the front of the room where they sat cross-legged on red meditation pillows waiting for class to begin.

A few minutes later, Mahkta's assistant rang a soft chime calling the class to order. Mahkta shimmied her sexy ass up to the front of the room.

"In case we haven't met, I'm Mahkta Patel, founder and director of *Erotic Journeys Institute*. You've all been briefed on what to expect today. I ask only that you remain open, despite any discomfort or embarrassment you might feel."

What the hell had Merrill gotten her into this time?

Mahkta took a sip of water and continued her litany, "I begin our studies with *Nyasa*. *Nyasa* is an ancient practice of Tantric medicine that teaches us to recognize and acknowledge the interconnectedness of all things."

"Through Nyasa, I will show you how to turn you and your lover's body into one divine entity. You will also begin to master what makes a body come alive. You see, it is not just touch that moves us. It's the emotions behind the touch. The way our bodies rise to meet our lover's fingers. The slight pain when our partner grabs our hair or spanks our bottom. All is *Nyasa*. All is Tantric Medicine."

Kalina found herself captivated by Mahkta's words. She felt like magic dust had been sprinkled over her head. Mahkta continued to work her mojo.

"I need a volunteer. One brave soul who is ready to experience something incredible. Someone who is ready to be completely vulnerable with the person they love."

Twelve out of thirteen hands shot up like somebody had lit a firecracker beneath their seats. Kalina's hand was the only one flat on her lap.

Mahkta looked around the room for her subject. Her eyes settled on a man in a burgundy sweat suit with a white tank underneath. Merrill Steven Santiago. The love of

Kalina's life. She'd loved that man since the day she met him at the library checking out books on how to save the planet.

Merrill went to the front of the class and stretched out on a white couch whose shape mimicked a human body. Mahkta instructed him to close his eyes and take his mind someplace relaxing. After he obeyed, she slid up his shirt exposing perfectly chiseled abs. She picked up a bottle of oil that had been warming in a bowl of heated water. She saturated her hands and massaged the oil over Merrill's skin.

Kalina watched for Merrill's reaction to Mahkta's warm, soft hands. Five minutes and seventeen strokes later, Merrill's body started to respond.

Mahkta's instructions continued. "It's not always about touching an area that is considered a high arousal zone. Focus on sending your vibration into the body of your lover."

Kalina wanted to kick Mahkta's ass. She was irritated with Merrill too. Why would he volunteer to let another woman touch him in front of a class full of strangers? She shot up out of her chair, fully prepared to go up there and get

her husband off that couch. Mahkta beat her to the punch...

"Perfect! We have another volunteer. Kalina, please

join me at the teaching platform."

Slick. That Mahkta was cunning. She must've known she

was about to get her ass put in check, Kalina thought to herself.

Kalina sashayed her dime piece body up to the front

of the classroom. She wanted Mahkta to see what Merrill had

waiting at home. Wanted her to know they had no need for a

class in intimacy, touch or anything else that had to do with

sex.

Merrill kept his eyes closed tight. Like he knew if

their eyes met, he'd have to acknowledge the anger and

questions brewing in Kalina's heart.

Mahkta took Kalina's hand in her hand and massaged

Merrill's stomach. She made Kalina drag her nails lightly

across his abs before she let go. When Merrill let out a soft moan, the women in the room shifted in their seats. The heat was starting to rise and circulate between the walls of *Erotic Journeys.*

"Ah yes, Kalina. You're doing great. Now I want you to close your eyes and let your heart guide your hands and fingers. Don't worry, I will be standing nearby to keep you grounded."

Kalina slowly closed her eyes.

"Hold out your hands." Mahkta told her as she poured more of the warm oil into her palms.

"I want you to rub the oil on his belly. Start slow and gentle and then merge into deep, long strokes."

Kalina followed her directions.

A few minutes later, Merrill was moaning out of control. As much as she wanted to end their little performance, Kalina didn't want to disappoint Merrill.

Mahkta intervened. "Kalina, I want you to open your eyes and tell me what you see."

Kalina looked down at her husband. His caramel skin was flushed. His palms were sweating. Her eyes traveled downtown to the Candy Man. It was hard as a rock.

"Are you surprised at how turned on your husband is by the simple art of touch?"

She wasn't sure how to answer that question so she settled on honesty. "A little. He usually likes....he usually gets like this when I put my mouth on him."

Giggles from the class erupted.

"Now you have a second pair of lips. Or shall we say a third pair of lips." Mahkta said with a chuckle.

"As much as I give him, a third pair couldn't hurt." Kalina told her. She said it as a statement, an assurance that she knew how to take care of her man and didn't need some sex therapist telling her what to do.

"Would you like to take him into the love chamber and relieve a little pressure?"

Merrill was embarrassed. He spoke up before she could answer. "I'm fine. Just point me to some cold water."

Mahkta directed him to the bathroom. Kalina trailed closely on his heels.

In the bathroom she grilled him. "I'm wondering if the schoolboy has a crush on his teacher? I thought we were coming here to experience what we're going to offer at *Destiny Awakened*. Now I'm not so sure."

Merrill looked over at his wife. Her golden brown hair with blonde highlights. Her bronze skin, high cheekbones and full lips.

He peered at how her red dress hugged her magnificent breasts and stallion legs like a wet suit. He wondered how she could doubt his love or his loyalty. He darn near worshipped her.

"What are you talking about, Kalina? You are and always will be the only woman I want to love."

"Why this class? Why now?"

"We've been together five years. The sex is still amazing. We're here because I want to keep it that way. With our business taking off and me being gone so much, I want our time together to be mind-blowing."

Kalina was instantly sorry she'd said such callous words. Her husband just wanted to strengthen what they had. She felt the need to make it up to him. She dropped to her knees right there on the bathroom tile.

"You're still hard. Was it my touch that made him this happy?"

"You have to ask?"

She took what was hers out of his pants. She let her mouth encircle it then ran her tongue up and down it.

She flicked her tongue underneath the head then sucked it deep into her mouth. She sucked and licked him like that for a few minutes until she had that cobra's full attention.

Merrill was in heaven. "Yeahhhh....suck that Daddy Long Stroke. Feels good. Hot oil....you rubbing my stomach....so close to the cobra....in front of all those people. That shit got me turned on. Mmm, that feels good, Kalina."

She stopped playing around and gave him what she knew he wanted. She deep-throated his entire snake. Moved her mouth up and down him like she was eating a strawberry popsicle. Merrill moaned, let his head roll back and surrendered to her hoodoo.

"Oh God, Kalina. You're fucking gonna make me come."

He reached underneath her dress, wiggled his fingers beneath her panties to her wetness, let his index finger slide into her.

"Keep sucking it, baby. Don't stop....."

He fingered her while she sucked, heightened the intensity of his building orgasm.

Two fingers later, Merrill was seconds away from an atomic bomb. He added a third finger to Kalina's ecstasy. He squeezed and teased her swollen love button with his thumb and index finger while he pumped his other three fingers in and out of her. She sucked the cobra like she was extracting venom from it.

"Oh God, Kalina. Shit....baby. Don't stop....Daddy Long Stroke is coming...coming for you."

Kalina felt her orgasm rising too. As if on cue, the room beside them broke out into applause at the exact moment Kalina and Merrill's bodies were racked with deep, titillating throbs that made them curl over to endure the pleasure.

"Merrill....I'm coming. Coming so...fucking....hard."

They sat there on the floor of the bathroom, leaning on each other, panting like they'd run a marathon, bodies throbbing out of control. Kalina nestled her face into

61

Merrill's neck. That affection merged into a long, deep, passionate kiss.

Merrill spoke first. "Damn baby, that was...amazing. Did I dispel your doubts?"

"Yeah, I guess you did. I'm not done with you but we better get back to class."

She smoothed down her dress, rinsed her mouth out, refreshed her face with a paper towel and a bit of soap. Merrill zipped up his jacket, washed her love off his hands and straightened out his sweat pants.

When they emerged from the bathroom, Mahtka was finishing the last exercise. She smiled knowingly at them as they took their seats.

"Ahhh, proof that my touch theory works. By the ruby red color on your cheeks, I believe your bodies answered the erotic call."

It was a statement not a question.

Kalina was a little embarrassed at being called out like that. She smiled, nodded and prayed Mahkta would move on.

After class was over, Mahkta called Kalina over to her desk.

"I watched you earlier with your husband. You're very loving and attentive. But I sense that while you've mastered the art of loving him, you haven't fully surrendered your own vulnerability. That could signal there's a few trust issues. I can help you fix it. But it'll take all the courage you can summon to get to the other side."

"I'm not necessarily agreeing with you about the vulnerability thing or saying yes to letting you help me but I'm open to hearing more."

"Unfortunately, I can't tell you very much. Part of the surrendering process at *Erotic Journeys* has to do with embracing the mystery. The reason sensuality in a marriage slows down is because the mystique diminishes. Even the

63

most creative lovers can sometimes run out of ways to surprise each other.

Fortunately, there's always another level of intimacy. Always a way to go deeper with our emotions and the expression of love."

"Go on."

"Tomorrow night, one of my students is hosting a private gathering."

"What kind of gathering?"

"It's an overnight affair designed to help you connect with the energy of *Nyasa*. They do this by uncovering and clearing your blocks to experiencing intimacy. *Erotic Journeys* is a sponsor for the event. It's not cheap but from the testimonies of those who've attended, I believe it's worth every dollar."

"Interesting."

Mahkta wrote down a phone number on the back of a business card and handed it to her.

"The password for this week's event is *Journeys*. Text the organizers at that number. Give them your name, my last name and the password. They will text you the address and other pertinent information. Remember to *only* send my last name."

"Hold on—this isn't one of those sex club things is it? If this is about hanging out with a bunch of swingers, I'm not interested. I'm very happy in my marriage and there's no way I'm bringing chaos and craziness into my home for the sake of an orgasm."

Mahkta seemed unmoved by Kalina's emotional outburst. "It's not a sex club. That I can tell you for sure. But do wear something that expresses your divineness. Everything else is provided. And take your appetite. I hear the food is scrumptious!"

Kalina exhaled and tried to regain her composure. "Mahkta, let me be up front with you. I'm not sure this is right for me. But I'll talk to Merrill and let you know what we decide. What's the name of the event? Just in case they have more than one."

"They call it the *Sleepover*. And it's only for women. It's the only..."

"Just women? Okay, this definitely isn't going to work. This sister here is strictly dickly. All day long. 365 days a...."

"...As I was saying, the men come later, after the sessions are over. And I repeat, Kalina, it's not about the sex. It's about the surrender. Try to keep an open mind. But whatever you decide, we here at *Erotic Journeys* support you."

Kalina walked off fully intending to tear up the card Mahkta had written the event info on. There was no way she was attending some lesbian sleep-over with a bunch of carpet munching bitches that hadn't been with a man in twenty years. What could they, of all people, teach her about improving her marriage?

In the car, Merrill knew something was wrong. Kalina was quiet almost the entire ride home.

"Kalina, what's wrong? And remember I know you—so don't lie to me."

"Mahkta invited me to some *Sleep Over* event. A bunch of women doing God knows what to help them become more sexually surrendered. Bottom line, I'm not interested."

"I understand." Merrill knew better than to try to convince her.

"I mean, what could a group of gay hens teach me about loving my man?"

"How do you know they're gay? And maybe it's not about your *man*. Maybe there's something there for you."

"I'm not letting a single one of those bitches near you."

"Kalina, we already talked about this. I'm not trying to bring another woman into our marriage. Where's the insecurity coming from?"

"I just...Just don't know what I'd get out of doing something like this."

"And you'll never know unless you check it out."

"So you're telling me I should go?"

"I'm not *telling* you anything. All I'm saying is, Mahkta seems like cool people and she definitely knows her stuff. She's worked with hundreds of couples and—have you read the testimonies on her web site?"

"I don't want to talk about it anymore. I'm hungry. Take me get something to eat."

Merrill took her cue and changed the subject.

"What do you have a taste for?" He asked smiling hopefully.

"I already had my fill of that." Kalina's anger cooled a bit when she thought about their fun in the bathroom at *Erotic Journeys*.

"How about fish?" Merrill said, with a gleam in his eye.

"Oh, you want some of this now, huh?"

"Hell yeah. I always want some of that."

"If you feed me and don't mention the name Mahkta Patel for the next few hours, you might just get lucky."

"Sounds like a deal to me."

They drove up the coast toward Laguna Beach and had dinner at one of their favorite seafood joints. They dined on King Crab Legs and broiled fish. They ate, laughed and talked until the night staff informed them the restaurant was about to close.

After dinner, they bought cheap wine, chocolate candy and plastic cups at the corner liquor store. They parked near the pier overlooking the water, sipped wine and fed each other dark chocolate.

It was Kalina who reopened the conversation about *Erotic Journeys*.

"Your *best friend* Mahkta told me I'm not fully surrendering when we have sex. She said I need to learn how to be more vulnerable with you. I think it's some bull. Just a way to get a shitload of money out of us for something we can do on our own."

"Well, what they offer isn't really that expensive. If you check it out and its crap, leave. It's not gonna hurt us for you to check it out."

"What if they wanna tie me up and eat my pussy?"

"Can I watch?" Merrill asked cracking up laughing.

"You got jokes, huh?"

"Look, if you go and don't like what they're doing, I'll send a car for you. You come home. We have a good laugh and put it all behind us."

"Fine. I might check it out. In the meantime, show me how much you love me."

She lifted her legs and let them rest on his lap. He slid off her shoes and tossed them onto the back seat. He massaged her feet until her body relaxed. When he had her where he wanted her, he raised her left leg, wrapped it around the back of his neck and inched her hips up toward his lips.

Merrill slid her panties to the side and took her into his mouth. He nibbled, sucked and licked on her flesh then tongued-fucked her for a little while. Stuck his taste buds deep inside her cave until she was almost screaming.

"You're holding back, Kalina. Let go and let me love you."

She relaxed and let her legs fall open.

He used his lips to kiss, stretch and lightly pull on her love button.

"Yes…..mmmm. Just like that. Don't stop, baby."

71

He sucked her like a lollipop, smacked on her jewels like he was eating a bowl of chocolate ice cream.

"Now you're being a good girl."

He slapped her ass. Turned his head sideways and licked that kitty kat until it was purring in his mouth.

"Ahhhh….yeah…eat this pussy, baby. You know….you know how I like it."

He slapped her ass four times. Made it sting real good. Then he anchored her clit between his tongue and top teeth, put his tongue under the fleshy pearl and moved his lips in an ocean-like motion. In, out, suck, lick, release. He repeated the process until Kalina went nuts.

"You fucking got it, baby. Don't stop, Merrill. I'm gonna fucking come for you."

He slid his middle and index fingers inside of her. He kept sucking her like a cool piece of ice between his lips. He felt her losing it.

"Give it to me, Kalina. Give me all of you. Come in Daddy's mouth."

She started screaming.

"Got damnit Merrill, I'm coming for you!"

He felt her treasure box contracting on his tongue. She climaxed so hard her body jacked-knifed then flipped around like a fish out of water. He held her in a vice grip until he sucked all of the come out of her body.

She backed away from him, got up on her knees and straddled him. Her ass was against the steering wheel. She snatched his pants down, rammed Daddy Long Stroke inside of her and started riding it like a bronco.

"God, you are so wet, Kalina. So wet and so hot."

She arched her back against the steering wheel and bounced up and down on his lap.

"So fucking turned on. Needed this so much." She told him in a passionate whisper.

73

"You're gonna make me come too fast. Slow down, Kalina."

"I can't. I'm so....so hot, baby. You feel so good. Just take it. Take this pussy hard and fast."

He understood what she was saying. She needed him to be a little beasty with her. He gripped her hips and started moving her ass up, down and around in a circle.

"Oh shit...mmmm...Kalina....dayum....so good. So fucking good."

"Yes, Merrill. Give me all of that juicy dick. Every fucking inch."

"Take it, baby. Take all of it."

"Come all over my ass. I want to feel it dripping down my back."

She slammed her body down onto him again and again. When he was ready to come, she let his dick slide out and onto her ass. She felt his warm nectar on her back.

"Ahhhhhhhh, fuck yeah, Kalina. That's good. So fucking good."

She slid his dick back into her and let her pussy drink the last of his honey.

She was whimpering, loving the feeling of his warmth on her back and his erection filling her up on the inside.

When their passion had waned, she moved from his lap onto the seat beside him.

She leaned over and kissed him on the cheek.

"Thank you, baby. Now I feel better."

He reached under the seat and gave her a towel for her back.

"Kalina, look at me. Look me in the eyes."

He was still slightly out of breath from their loving. He turned her face toward his.

"Our marriage is fine. You're a great wife and a wonderful lover."

"Good. Let's go home. I guess I have to pack for an erotic journey."

At home Kalina showered and slipped into bed. There was little talking as her mind was on the experience she'd agreed to embark on the following morning.

***

She woke to vision of Merrill's thick muscular body standing before the bathroom mirror. His bottom half was covered by a plush green towel. His back still had droplets of water from his morning shower. She watched him rinse and dry his freshly shaven face then style his curly black hair to perfection.

He bent down and kissed her lips on the way out of the door. His manly smell was so intoxicating she wanted to pull him down on top of her and have her way.

"I guess I'll see you tomorrow?" He asked planting his soft thick lips on hers.

"Yeah, I guess so. But keep your cell on and your driver ready. I may need an intervention."

"You'll be fine, Kalina. This I know."

"If you say so."

"I'll see you soon my beautiful wife."

She called out after him. "You need anything else for the opening next week? I called the caterer yesterday and added two more vegetarian dishes. I also booked Jay Boykin, the sax player. They're gonna love him."

"We're good. You go have a great time. And relax. Promise me you'll relax."

"I promise."

After Merrill left, Kalina ran herself a hot bath. While she soaked her mind ran over a myriad of scenes of what might happen during the Sleepover.

She imagined a group of women chillaxing in a swimming pool sized Jacuzzi. One by one they took off their clothes. She pictured their breasts surrounding her. Felt their tongues and lips all over her body. She found herself getting turned on and that scared her. She rose from the water, dried off and packed the rest of her clothes before fear kept her home.

Ninety minutes and some change later, Merrill's driver drove her up to the gate of a fabulous Hollywood mansion. Kalina exhaled her nervousness as Francois pulled up to the speaker so she could give the password.

"Santiago. Journeys. Patel." She said into the speaker.

The gate rolled open. Francois glided down the driveway to the front door while Kalina's heart darn near beat out of her chest.

A liveried butler met them at the circular driveway. He helped her from the car and took her rolling bag inside.

Kalina had chosen Fuschia leggings, a black leather halter and a hot pink feathery vest for her date with *Erotic Journey*. Thigh high boots with rhinestone encrusted toes and heels set her ensemble on fire. Her curly brown-blonde curls bounced as she walked.

She moved through the foyer into a massive living room with red walls and white furniture. The stark contrast of the two colors jolted her and made her feel deliciously excited.

A drop-dead gorgeous Black woman wearing an indigo pants suit welcomed her inside. Her sun-baked skin and freckled cheeks looked wholesome and appealing. She was rocking one of those blonde Beyonce weaves and it was working for her big time.

"Kalina Santiago. Welcome to our monthly sleepover. I'm Regina Evans-Richards, wife of NBA B-ball player, Stephon Richards and founder of B-girl Cosmetics. I'm also the ambassador for this gathering."

"Nice to meet you, Regina. How'd you know who I was?"

"Oh—they send us pictures of the guests to ensure we have the right people."

"So that's why they had me send a picture when I registered."

Regina's phone chimed with a text message. After she checked it she said, "Why don't you go ahead and get settled in. Dinner will be served in thirty minutes. There's juice, sparkling water and champagne—whatever floats your boat. Some of your E.J. sisters are already here. We're still waiting on a few others. Make yourself at home."

"E.J. Sisters? What's that?"

"Erotic Journeys Sisters."

Kalina nodded. "Oh, right. Where's your lady's room?"

Regina pointed down the hall.

Back in the Great Room, Kalina lifted a glass of champagne from the butler's silver tray. She put it to her lips then put it back on the tray.

She decided she wanted to stay sober for a while. At least until she figured out what the hell was going down at this women only bashorama.

She looked around the room at the other guests. Felt relieved at how upscale they all seemed. They were dressed to the nines, had fabulous hair, shoes and purses. Their conversations were mostly about their businesses and the projects they were launching. At first glance, the *Sleepover* was nothing more than a professional networking circle.

A few minutes later, Regina called everybody to order. Kalina counted five other women in addition to her and Regina.

"Greetings EJ Sisters. I'm delighted to welcome you to the *Journey Mansion*. Over the next twenty four hours, we will embark on the adventure of a lifetime. Right now we're going to introduce ourselves, share a little about what we do and why we're here. Then my chef is going to serve an incredible meal that will awaken every taste bud on your tongue."

She took a sip of champagne and continued.

"Your luggage has already been moved to your suite. And while each of you has your own living space, keep in mind that at any time, another sister can and may join you in your room to talk, share and learn. Understood?"

Everybody nodded their heads.

"The Sleepover is an opportunity for you to get to know yourself better and to explore your desires on deeper levels. We employ ancient Tantric medicine as a means to help you achieve this goal. Know that we've been trained to keep you safe and happy throughout your time with us. We take our jobs very serious."

One of the sisters raised her hand with a question.

"Can we leave if we want to?"

"Yes, you are free to go at any time. But so far, in ten years of doing this work, no woman has ever left during one of our gatherings."

Regina held up a stack of papers. "We have signed non-disclosures and confidentiality agreements from each of you. Other than that, there are only two rules for this retreat. If it feels good, go with it. If it doesn't feel good, end it. We've found that if we honor these two rules, everything else will work itself out."

Regina glanced at a text message and finished her welcome speech. "Each of you has an individual helper to answer your questions, get whatever you want or need. We feel that all women should, at one time in their lives, have everything they want. Even if it's just for a day."

Everyone nodded their heads in agreement.

"Okay. Please introduce yourselves as I call your names. Tell us a little about what you do and why you're here. Bettina, would you go first?"

"Sure. I'm Bettina Caraville. I was born in Spain but grew up in America. My husband is CEO of *SDS Communications*, the firm that owns most of the cell phone towers in this country. I teach wellness seminars across the country and just had my first book picked up by *Random House*. It's called *Stupid Crazy Sexy Body*. It hits bookstores next week. I'm here because Mahkta Patel and I have been friends for many years and she thought my attending would help me do my work as a wellness coach more efficiently."

Kalina thought Bettina's Spanish accent was sexy as hell. Her thick blonde mane made her look like a model for a shampoo commercial.

"Thank you, Bettina. Evelyn, you're next."

"I'm Evelyn Bordeaux. Originally from New Orleans now living in Los Angeles. I own *Love Pleasures*, an on-line adult store that sells high end sex toys. Last year LP made the *Forbes* list of Fortune 500 corporations. I'm married to William Lenover, CEO of *Lenover Electronics*. I'm a mom of two and I love to travel. I think I lost myself somewhere between being a mom and being a wife. I'm here to get me back."

Evelyn reminded Kalina of Paula Patton, the beautiful Mulatto who was married to that handsome actor and singer, Robin Thicke. Evelyn's southern accent made her seem innocent and coy. But Kalina had a feeling there was a wild cat hiding behind that sweet voice and petite body.

Regina pointed at a full-figured sister with a short Halle Berry haircut. "Sophia, the mic's in your hand."

"I'm Sophia Miller. My husband owns *Miller Real Estate* conglomerate. I have a degree in interior design and have worked with everybody from Oprah to John Legend. I'm here because I think my husband's getting bored with me. I think it's my weight. I've tried everything but can't lose more than a couple of pounds."

"You're gorgeous, Sophia. Stunning is more like it." Regina told her. "But it's not how the world sees us—it's how we see ourselves. That's what *Erotic Journeys* is all about. Loving ourselves just as we are. Thank you, Sophia. Chantrel, it's your turn."

"Chantrel Migliato here. I was born in Italy. I came to America to pursue my dream of becoming a sports model. I've worked for *Nike, Puma, Fila*—let's just say if its sports related—my face and body helped endorse it. I'm here because there's something….or someone that pulling at my heart. My family and my partner….let's just say they don't mix. I'm here for direction on which way to let my heart move."

Chantrel was model tall, had runners legs and breast implants that Kalina knew must've cost a mint. Her smile was dentist perfect. Her skin was as smooth as porcelain.

Regina smiled and said, "Your heart already knows the answer, Chantrel. But we'll help you catch up with it. Kalina, you have the floor."

"I'm Kalina Santiago. My husband and I are in the process of opening, *Destiny Awakened*, our new day spa. I made my money through a line of national shoe outlets which I sold to one of the big guys for triple my investment."

"I guess I'm here to learn how to become more emotionally and sexually vulnerable with my husband. I'm not sure how this retreat will help with that but I'm willing to give it a try."

"Splendid. Sounds good, Kalina. Ayo, why don't you close us out."

Kalina thought Ayo had the body of an African goddess. Her nails and toes were painted a fierce pink and adorned with rhinestones. The pink was a sexy contrast to her ebony skin. As she spoke, a menagerie of brass bangles jingled on her left wrist.

"I am Ayo Olusuro. I hail from Nigeria, West Africa, by way of Hollywood. I'm what they call a blockbuster screenwriter. *Dreamworks* just optioned my third screenplay. I love sex but I hate love. Love makes you open to being hurt and I'm tired of having my heart trampled on. I'm here to learn how to stop being hurt by the men I love."

Regina intervened.

"Love, my dear Ayo, is not supposed to hurt. Not if it's authentic."

Ayo nodded quietly.

"Okay, ladies. That's good for now. It's time to indulge our tongues and tummies in some delectable goodies."

Regina held up her index finger like she was checking the temperature and motioned them to follow. As Kalina made her way toward the dining room, she thought about the women of Erotic Journeys.

Bettina. Evelyn. Sophia. Chantrel. Ayo.

All intelligent, ambitious women with powerhouse men and top-shelf careers. Kalina thought perhaps she might've been wrong about *Erotic Journeys*. Maybe it wasn't a sex club. But she couldn't help but wonder what had driven them to a place like this? She had come because she felt Merrill wanted her to. She seriously doubted she would've come on her own. She wondered again what moved five beautiful, successful sisters to attend a gathering like *Erotic Journeys?*

Kalina glanced at her watch. One hour down, twenty-three more to go.

Dinner was lemon-garlic prawns, peanut tofu, a scrumptious spinach salad with cranberries, coconut jasmine rice and strawberry vegan cheesecake. Chef Stephanie was incredibly talented. Just like Mahkta said the food was beyond delicious.

After dinner they took showers and changed into their night clothes. Some of her EJ sisters took the pajama thing really serious. Kalina had never seen that much designer sleeping gear in one room. As sexy as it was, a lot of it could've doubled as night club wear.

They hiked past the pool, through the state of the art work-out facility, past a huge dance floor, to a twenty-five seat movie theater.

They watched an old classic, *Love Jones,* one of Kalina's favorite chick flicks and munched on cheddar-flavored popcorn. The sexy love scenes in the movie had her and her EJ sisters twitching in their seats.

After the movie was over, Kalina noticed Regina had tipped away. One the helpers escorted them back to the main house. When they walked into the living room, their eyes bulged with surprise. The *Sleepover* activities had escalated a few thousand degrees…

Kalina eyes and body went into overload as she took in the entire scene.

There were scented candles burning in every corner. Two adult-sized cages with leather bar stools were on each side of the room. Long white couches with curves that matched the human body and red velvet covered chairs were strategically placed throughout the space. Two massive

jacuzzi's bubbled front and center.

One of those seductive *Buddha Lounge* CD's played

over the speaker system. Fragrant smoke rose from the

puffing end of six Hookah pipes. A full bar was set up in the

corner that featured the best alcoholic sin on the market.

Kalina noticed that Regina had changed into her

leathers. Her borderline S&M gear made her look like she

was ready to whoop some ass.

"Welcome Sisters. We have a fab evening planned

for you. Please help yourself to drinks, food, whatever you

desire. If you don't see it, let us know and we'll get it for

you."

Each of them found a space to chill in the

humungous room. Regina's helpers passed out slips of paper

and writing tools along with a small clip board. Kalina's

hand slightly shook as she accepted her tools.

It wasn't fear that made her hands shake. It was anticipation. A fire was brewing between her legs and she didn't know why, neither could she stop it. Truth be told, she didn't want it to stop.

"One of the most important steps in your *Erotic Journey* is getting in touch with your innermost desires."

"We begin this work by tapping into what Mahkta calls *Pranah* in Tantric Medicine. We've created a special exercise to assist you with this. Begin by writing down three fantasies. Three erotic dreams that end with you in a state of total bliss."

Regina strolled slowly through the room peering into their eyes as she spoke. Her leather suit hugged the curves of her body like a glove. Her thigh high boots pimped out her onion booty. She stopped directly in front of Kalina and spoke as if she were talking only to her.

"You must release any fear or shame you carry about your desires. Dig deep inside yourself and ask your Spirit

92

what it wants. We're going to provide a little stimulation to help you tune inward. Remember the two rules. If it feels good, go with it. If it doesn't feel good, end it. Also remember, you are safe here. No one will ever ask you to do anything that doesn't feel good. Now write! Don't stop writing until your spiritual pen is empty."

A litany of sensual music began to play over the stereo system. A long line of women with killer bodies wearing blindfolds, colored thongs and sexy lace bras were ceremonially led into the room. They stood in front of them like they were on display. The helpers stepped up behind them and remove their blindfolds.

A couple of the women entered the cages. Others sunk down into steaming Jacuzzis or crouched on the large red pillows. The women danced erotically, played with each other's bodies and teased the guests of *Erotic Journeys*. A few slid their hands up and down their shiny skin. Some did things so freaky Kalina had to turn her head.

93

Sweet amber incense burned in copper holders. A silver tray bearing bowls of honey, saucers with mangos, cherries, pineapple drizzled with chocolate and fresh peaches was carried in by a woman in a Black leather thong and matching bra.

The woman with the tray offered each of them something from her array of treats. When she bent down, her breasts bubbled forward almost exposing her dark sexy nipples.

Kalina licked her lips, swallowed and tried to gather herself. She looked around the room at her EJ sisters. Each had a dazed look in her eye. Like a spell had been cast over them rendering them speechless, unable to move or talk.

Just when Kalina thought it couldn't get any deeper, there was a loud crunching sound. The walls in the room began to slide open. Behind the large wall that their seats were facing, there was a whole other room. A secret compartment...

In the secret room, beautiful waterfalls poured from the ceiling into small ponds. A skylight gave them an incredible view of sparkling stars glowing against a midnight sky. There was a movie screen running footage of an ocean crashing onto the shore.

To the right of the movie screen was a mechanical horse covered in red velvet. He had a huge, lifelike dildo attached near the spot where you mounted him. He was bucking in slow motion to the beat of the music. His movements were insanely erotic.

In the center of the room on a makeshift stage was a satin and lace covered stripper pole. A woman wearing a pink maid uniform sashayed across the stage and curled her thick legs around it. Her pink fishnets were held up with a red garter. Her shiny pink stilettos made her feet look like candy. She wore no panties and her yoni was completely shaved.

The Italian sports model, Chantrel Migliato, was the first one to rise to her feet. She took baby steps toward the woman in pink. When the woman saw her approaching, she semi-ran then leapt onto the stripper's pole. She did a somersault, flipped upside down and descended the pole in a scissor position all the way down to the floor. Kalina watched Chantrel's knees buckle as she reached over and touched the woman's right leg.

The woman commenced to performing an erotic display of what Regina informed us was Tantric dancing on Chantrel's behalf.

Regina clapped her hands as if to applaud Chantrel's courage. She yelled her encouragement. "Take all you want, Chantrel. You can have whatever you desire tonight."

Bettina, the author and wellness coach joined one of the thong wearing women on a red pillow. The woman made Bettina lay back on the pillow while she painted her body with the sweet red juice from a ripe cherry. When she finished painting, she used her tongue to clean up the remainder.

Sophia, the full-figured sister with the Halle Berry haircut was the next among them to find her courage.

She made her way over to one of the cages. She had a bowl of honey in her right hand. The woman in the cage crawled over to her. She reached through the bars, dipped her finger in Sophia's honey bowl and sucked that sweet nectar off her fingers. Kalina saw Sophia's body shutter when the woman did that.

The woman dipped her fingers in the honey a second time. This time she fed Sophia her honey. Sophia sucked the woman's fingers clean. When she'd had her fill, she opened the door to the cage and stepped inside.

Kalina saw where this was going. She wanted to get out of there before she was the last woman on the couch, the *only* woman refusing to participate in this high priced sex fest.

Regina, like she was reading her mind, sat down next to Kalina.

"Kalina, where are your fantasies? Your page is blank my sister."

Regina placed her hand over Kalina's heart which was beating as hard as a thousand drums.

"*Nyasa.* Open your heart dear sister. Take off the chains and let it come out to play. It—your heart—holds the key to your vulnerability."

"I….I'm not gay. I don't like women like that. Nothing personal. Just not my thing."

Regina smiled. "This is not about being gay, Kalina. Come with me."

"Come with you or *come* with you?"

Regina cracked up at that one. "You're so funny, Kalina. I've already had my *Erotic Journey.* This is *your* weekend. Okay, how about *follow* me? Is that better? But you can *come* too if that's what makes you feel good."

Regina led her to the horse.

She tapped Kalina's ass lightly. "Giddy up. He won't bite. I promise."

Kalina's pajamas were a black two piece shorts and camisole set with a matching robe. She wore no panties beneath the shorts. Not exactly riding gear.

"I...I'm not dressed for this."

"Does it look like the others are concerned with what you're wearing?"

Kalina looked around at the rest of her EJ sisters.

Bettina was in the Jacuzzi sipping Cognac and being fed fruit by two of the thong-wearing sisters. Ayo was on the body-shaped couch being massaged by three people and six hands. Evelyn, the southern belle, was sitting on the couch waiting to see what she and Regina were getting ready to do. Chantrel was nursing the hell out of a dirty martini and sucking on a Hookah like her life depended on it. The lady in pink was beside her.

"Come on, Kalina. We don't have all night."

Kalina untied her robe, put her left leg into the stirrup and swung her right leg over the back of the horse.

"I'm not putting that….that thing inside of me."

"Not required. Only there as an option."

Regina picked up what looked like a remote control and pressed a button. The horse began to buck slowly. It also began to vibrate.

"Whoa. This thing is vibrating."

"We call him William. And yes, he has his own vibrational rhythm. Just relax and take the ride. Let me know if it stops feeling good."

Merrill had told her to relax. Kalina summoned her courage from someplace deep inside and tried to enjoy the experience.

Unlike the bucking broncos Kalina had seen in the movies, this one didn't spin around. She held on as the horse gently rocked her pelvis forward and backwards. Her hands naturally gravitated to the penis as a means to keep her balance.

When she went forward, her pearl pulsated with the machine's vibration. When she rocked backwards, the vibrations traveled upward to her g-spot. The deep sensation of the dual stimulation was what drew her in and ultimately got her.

After a few minutes of the red horse's rocking and vibration, she realized she'd gotten aroused. She was about to call Regina over to turn him off so she could get down. Before she could summon her, Evelyn made a request in her petite southern voice that caught her off guard.

"Kalina, is it? Your name?"

"Yes. Kalina."

"Would you mind terribly if I piggy backed on your ride?"

"Uh…actually, you can have him. I was just about to get down."

"No, please stay. I....I'm feeling a little out of place here and it'd be nice to have a friend to talk to."

Kalina didn't want to assume anything. Maybe Evelyn just wanted a little company.

"You know this thing vibrates, right?"

"It...it's cool. I'll just hop on the back. Is it fun?"

"Good exercise I guess. They say horseback riding is good for your legs."

The way the horse was designed—the deep dip of his back—it put Evelyn's pelvis directly on Kalina's butt. Once Evelyn was on board, William started to buck again. Evelyn had to hold Kalina around her waist to keep from falling off.

"Oh shit! This thing is really starting to rock." Evelyn said laughing.

Kalina laughed too. It was the first time all evening that she'd loosened up.

"You better hold on. I think Regina has a remote control and is making this thing speed up."

William made their bodies rock and swing in synchronicity. Now Kalina could feel Evelyn's breasts on her back. The faster William rocked, the tighter Evelyn held on. It felt like she was riding her ass in slow motion.

She thought she was hearing things when she heard a low moan come out of Evelyn's throat.

"You okay back there?"

"This thing is vibrating my clit. Ohhhh….God…it feels so good."

Kalina was torn. She wanted to get off the horse but didn't want to mess up Evelyn's good time.

Evelyn moaned again, this time louder. "Yes. Oh God, yes!"

Kalina closed her eyes and decided to ride it out.

One of Evelyn's hands went to Kalina's breast. Kalina couldn't tell if it was on purpose or because the horse was throwing them around.

Suddenly, Evelyn grabbed the horse's reins. The horse jolted and made them lay forward. Kalina's pubic mound was now smashed against the vibrations. The first vestiges of orgasmic energy shot through her pelvis. She kept her eyes closed, wrapped her arms around the horse's neck and held on for dear life. She and Evelyn rocked and hummed, hummed and rocked. Five minutes later they were both moaning.

Kalina wanted to stop but the pleasure from the vibration kept her locked in the down position. Between Evelyn's soft breasts on her back and the vibrations from the horse, she found herself moving into a sensual space she'd reserved only for Merrill.

Regina started clapping and shouting. "Yes! Feel it. Feel the pleasure my sisters!"

"I think I'm….Oh God…coming….coming goddamnit! Fuck…oh shit. I'm coming!" Kalina said as her body pulsated again and again.

Evelyn was on fire too. "Ohhhhhh.....I'm coming too. Yes, yes!"

Like it knew what had just gone down, the horse's pace began to slow. When he got to an easy rock, Evelyn managed to climb around Kalina and slide her body down in front of her. She then inched down on the life-like penis. Now her back was to Kalina and her ass was between Kalina's legs.

"I....I've had enough." Kalina told her standing up and swinging her now trembling right leg up and off the horse.

As soon as Kalina got down, the horse started moving again. Come rained down Kalina's thighs as she stood back and watched Evelyn ride that dick like a champion. The horse starting moving faster and faster making Evelyn's pussy slam back and forth, on and off the penis.

Evelyn started screaming as multiple orgasms shot through her body like electricity. Kalina found herself getting turned on again. Even worse, she wished she hadn't gotten off the horse.

Regina eased up next to Kalina and took her hand in her hand.

"Did you finish writing out your three fantasies?"

Kalina exhaled, barely able to tear her eyes away from Evelyn and said, "Yes. I think I just finished living out one of them. I've always wanted to have an orgasm in front of a room full of people."

"Excellent! That's awesome. We're about to move into the portion of the gathering where we share our fantasies with each other. Why don't you join me in the main room?"

Back in the main room, Kalina was shocked to see Sophia on all fours getting her naked ass spanked by one of the thong-wearing girls. A second woman was beneath her lapping her nectar like it was the juice of the Gods.

Chantrel was sitting in front of the stage, legs gapped, watching the stripper masturbate. Chantrel was finger-fucking herself and was seconds away from a climatic rocket too.

"These women.....everybody seemed so sophisticated and conservative when we first got here." Kalina told Regina.

"The Tantra cares nothing about our worldly identities. It's here to unite us with the divine energy, to free us from the limitations of our earthly shells."

A few orgasms later, Regina clapped three times and called her grown and sexy girl party to order.

"Ladies, please join me in the sister circle for the third level of our *Erotic Journey*."

One by one, Bettina, Evelyn, Ayo, Chantrel, Sophia and Kalina joined Regina in the circle. The helpers had set up pillows for each of them to sit on. In the middle of the circle there was a long pink pillow surrounded by lavender scented candles.

In front of the pillows, on a low round table, were platters of sweet fruits, bars of chocolate and a steaming pot of something or other. Hand-painted tea cups and saucers and tiny jars of honey accompanied each pillow.

"Our chef has prepared a little something to help you focus during the next phase of our gathering. The pot contains our very own *Mango Passion* tea made with herbs that are specific to the awakening and healing of your divine self. Please add honey to your liking.

The helpers walked around the circle filling each woman's cup and offering them chocolate and fruit.

When they were all fed and quenched, Regina continued her directives. "At the beginning of our last session, I asked each of your write out three fantasies. Tonight—or shall we say—this morning, we're going to share some of those fantasies with each other. I encourage you to release any shame about what your body and soul craves for your erotic liberation. Now, with that said, who would like to start?"

Kalina was surprised when Sophia's hand went up. She'd been the quiet one among the group. Sophia starting speaking from where she was sitting in the circle but Regina stopped her.

"Sophia, please come to the center of the circle to the position of sisterly adoration. Every woman should know what it feels like to be the center of attention."

After she was seated, Sophia began again. "I never thought in a million years that I would allow a stranger, a woman at that, to make love to me in front of room full of women I just met."

A few tears came to her eyes but she choked them back. "Regina helped me understand the sacredness of my full body."

"She told me to stop calling myself fat and to understand that my body is a map of the pleasure and joy I've experienced. The woman who I let love me tonight—she must've whispered in my ear a thousand times, "Beautiful. You're so beautiful." I finally heard her. *My heart heard her.* I feel healed as a result."

Regina smiled knowingly. "And now it's time to share your fantasy. No shame."

Sophia unfolded a piece of paper. "My fantasy begins in the thick of night. I'm on the bus going home. I'm wearing a short black dress underneath a long trench coat. The bus is crowded and people are stacked on top of each other."

"I'm standing near the back door holding onto the rail above my head to keep from falling. I look up to see an extremely handsome man getting on the bus. He's wearing a suit and is very well put together from head to toe. He wiggles through the maze of people to where I'm standing. He grabs the rail above my head."

Sophia paused to take a sip of her tea.

"What happens after he grabs the rail, Sophia?" Regina asked her mercilessly.

"I put my ass on his crotch. I pretended it was an accident but it wasn't. When the bus jolts, my ass slams into his crotch. I feel him getting hard. I grind my ass into him in a way that lets him know I know what I'm doing. The elderly couple sitting in front of me is asleep. The others on the bus are too much in their own world to notice us."

Sophia swallowed and continued.

"I take his hand and slide it under my dress. He starts massaging my pussy on top of my panties. I spread my legs and encourage him to go deeper. He slips his hand beneath my panties and starts to finger fuck me right there in the middle of all those people. The way we're positioned, they can't see what he's doing with his hand.

He unzips his pants and slides his dick under my dress and inside of me. He brings his right hand around and starts to play with my clit. His movements are subtle but his

111

dick is so thick it feels incredible. I'm so turned on I come all over his hands."

"Sounds amazing." Regina tells her before dismissing her from the position of adoration. "I think you should put that in a book, Sophia. Have you done it yet? In real life I mean?"

"My husband—he said he's too well known to get on a public bus."

"You can always rent a bus and hire actors. *Erotic Journeys* can arrange that for you. Let's talk about that later my love. Okay, Evelyn, you're up next."

Evelyn sashayed her southern-born hips over to the seat of adoration. She nibbled on a few pieces of pineapple, drank a few sips of tea, took a few bites of chocolate and went at it.

"My fantasy takes place at a fire station. I'm the cook. I'm serving two sexy firemen and one firewoman their breakfast. I'm wearing a short sexy maid uniform. As I spoon my scrambled eggs onto the plate of one of the firemen, he slides his hand up my leg. He plays with my clit for a few minutes. I act like I don't notice. I move to the next man. He takes the pan of eggs from me, makes me bend over across the table. He spanks my ass right on the fleshy part. Makes my pussy vibrate with each slap. Then he gets down on his knees and sucks on my pearl. Gets me nice and wet."

"When he's done, I stand up and go to the woman. She sits me down on her lap. She finger fucks me while kissing and sucking my breasts. Oh my God. I can't believe I'm telling you guys this."

"No shame, Evelyn. Please continue." Regina reminded her.

"One of the other firemen clears the dishes off the table. He lies down on his back on the table and tells me to get on top of him. I climb up on him and slide down on his dick. The second fireman walks behind us. He starts playing with my clit and later, he puts his dick in my ass. The third one—the woman—she walks around to the other end of the table and makes me lick her clit. I'm fucking one of them, giving the woman oral sex and being fucked in the ass all at the same time. I feel incredibly powerful and in control. We all get off at the same time and it's amazing. I come so hard I think my hearts gonna stop."

Regina clasped her hands together and tells them, "I think we have the beginning of an anthology. You women are….you have already exceeded my hopes for your class. Let's see, whose next…."

Kalina was terrified of Regina picking her to go next. First off, she was insanely turned on by Sophia and Evelyn's stories. Her pussy was so wet that she was sure her panties would make a swishing sound if she got up. Fortunately, Regina called on Chantrel followed by Bettina.

Chantrel, the sports model, shared a powerful fantasy about making love on top of the Empire State Building. She and her boyfriend were standing on a platform in long winter coats. Her coat had a hole in the back of it—a hole large enough for her boyfriend's penis. While people walked around gawking at the views atop one of the tallest buildings in the world, Chantrel and her lover had orgasm after orgasm.

Bettina Caraville, the Latin diva, wellness coach and author, confessed her desire to screw the postman.

She gave the sisters blow by blow details of her favorite masturbation fantasy where the guy who delivers the mail ends up getting the blowjob of Lfe and then fucking her in every room of the house.

When Bettina finished, Regina's eyes pivoted around to Kalina and Ayo.

"Well, which of you wants to go next?"

Thankfully, Ayo raised her hand.

"My ex—he tried to break me. But in the end, I rose like the phoenix I am. My fantasy takes place in a dungeon.

115

My ex and his female lover are my slaves. They are there to serve me, cook for and feed me whatever I want to eat."

Hot tears roll down her face as she says, "I keep them on leashes. I make them suck my toes and serve me like a queen. I have a lot of fantasies with them as my slave. But my favorite is the one where I'm sitting in his lap like he's a human throne."

"What happens while you're on your throne, Ayo?" Regina asked her.

"As I sit on his lap, his dick is deep inside of me. His lover kneels before me and takes my pearl in her mouth. She sucks me while he fucks me. I spank her ass until she is begging me to let her come. I tell her not to come until I say she can or I will punish her. God, I'm getting turned on just telling you guys about it. I think I need to stop or…"

"Good for you, Ayo. You took your power back after your heart was broken. But you must take this a step further and cut away the barbed wire around your heart. Our pleasure is totally elevated when we experience it from a healed place. I would like to talk with you more about this after the gathering. Thank you, sister."

Kalina's palms were sweating. Could she summon the courage to tell them her deepest darkest fantasy?

"Kalina, we're waiting for you dear sister. Please come and occupy the seat of sisterly adoration."

"I.....I'm not sure I can do this."

Regina rose from her seat, walked over to Kalina and took her hand.

"I admire you, Kalina. Even in the midst of your fear, you came here. I have a gift for you. Something I've never given any of my students. Sit. Sit down before your sisters and receive your healing."

Kalina sat down with her legs crossed.

Before she realized what was happening, Regina had straddled her. Her sunset skin crisscrossed with Kalina's caramel-colored covering. Regina wrapped her legs around

117

Kalina's back and embraced her. They were in the center of the circle, breast to breast, Regina's yoni on her navel. Kalina could feel the warmth emanating from Regina's center. It felt so good. *So soothing.* Regina began to rock her.

"Feel me, dear sister. Let go and let my chi heal you."

Kalina closed her eyes and let Regina take her where she wanted her to go. When she opened her eyes again she realized tears were pouring from her eyes.

"Tell us what it is, Kalina. Tell us what hurt you." Regina whispered in her ear.

"I saw him! I saw my father cheating on my mother. That's when I decided I would never trust a man completely. And I never have."

"You must release that pain. Give it to me. I will take it and release it at the sacred altar. Then you will be able to know love in all its fullness."

"How….how do I release it?"

118

"You already have. All I needed was your willingness to let it go. Now it's time for you to tell us your fantasy. And you must never be ashamed of your desires again."

Regina rose, went to the waterfall and cleansed her body of Kalina's pain in the waterfall of sacred waters.

"I'm listening, Kalina. Tell us the daydream that gets you wet as a thousand raindrops."

Kalina wiped her face, opened her journal and told her sisters what she'd never told anyone.

"In my fantasy I'm working as a secretary at a college. I've had a crush on the principal for years. This day I come to work wearing a short yellow sundress and matching yellow sandals. I'm in the front office unpacking and stocking supplies when I drop a box of pencils. They roll all over the floor. I'm on my hands and knees picking them up. My back is to the principal's office. I purposely let her see that I don't have any panties on. She gets up from her desk and comes over to help."

"Don't stop now, Kalina. You're almost there. Free yourself."

"She reaches through my legs to grab a pencil. I put my hot, wet pussy down on her hand. Before I can move it away, she starts to play with me. I continue picking up pencils like I don't notice her touching me. She tickles my pearl, gets me super wet, until I'm sloshing. I don't want her to stop so I put my ass high in the air, pretend like I'm looking for pencils under the cabinet. She unbuttons her blazer and unzips her pants. I see that she is strapped. She takes her dick out and bounces it on my ass. I back my pussy up and let her enter me. We start fucking right there on the floor in the main office. I'm just about to come when suddenly the door opens and somebody comes into the office."

"She pulls her dick out and crawls away. I crawl in the other direction. The person calls out but doesn't see anybody so they leave."

Ayo crawled over to Kalina and poured her some tea. Evelyn and Chantrel slide across the floor and feed her fruit and chocolate. Bettina and Sophia begin to massage her shoulders.

This seem to make Regina happy. "I love it when my E.J. sisters support each other. This is the idea of our community. Kalina, you're not finished. Please continue."

With her E.J. sisters by her side, Kalina found the courage to go on.

"I go to her office with a file. Pretend nothing happened. She tells me to sit down, that she wants to talk to me."

"What does she say, Kalina?"

"She says she's always been attracted to me but because of her position, she didn't tell me about it. I tell her I understand and hand her the file. She tells me to wait, that she wants to check it for mistakes. I slide my chair around to her side of the desk. When I do that, she asks me to stand up

121

then she sits me down on her desk. I lie back on the desk and spread my legs. She gets down on her knees and starts licking and sucking me. And this woman…oh God, this woman can eat some pussy. I'm damn near about to come again when she stops and unbuckles her pants again. She slides into me, starts playing with my clit and fucking me at the same time. I wrap my legs around her back and….oh God….I come so good."

Kalina was so caught up in the story she didn't notice Bettina and Sophia had opened her robe and were now massaging her neck and back.

Kalina stretched out and let them work their way down her thighs to her legs and feet. While Bettina and Sophia massaged her feet, Ayo, Chantrel and Evelyn cuddled up next to her and covered her body with gentle caresses.

"God, that feels so good. So relaxing." Kalina told them. She leaned her head to the side so Sophia could get to her shoulders.

Evelyn—the same woman who rode the horse with her—decided to take their sisterly affection to the next level.

Evelyn placed soft kisses down Kalina's thighs while Ayo massaged her temples. Chantrel placed her warm body across Kalina's pelvis and rode her like a stallion.

"Ahhhhh....mmmm.....what....what are y'all doing?"

"Do you want them to stop, Kalina?" Regina asked.

Kalina was quiet for a minute.

"No....I don't think I do."

Chantrel scooted down, slid Kalina's shorts over her hips and let her tongue dance across Kalina's flesh.

"Mmmmm. That feels good. So good." Kalina moaned.

Chantrel sucked Kalina's flesh between her lips while Evelyn slid two fingers inside of her.

123

Kalina felt a breast on her cheek. She opened her eyes to see Sophia's succulence dangling near her tongue. Kalina took Sophia's breasts in her hand, kissed and sucked those crown jewels like a pro.

Kalina heard Bettina ask one of the helpers for something. A few minutes later, Bettina lifted Kalina's body up and slid beneath her.

Kalina felt a penis between her legs. She looked down and noticed that Bettina had gotten strapped. Chantrel, who was working her clit like a day job, guided that healthy piece of flesh inside of her while she continued sucking Kalina's clit.

Ayo, Sophia and Evelyn began to kiss and lick all over her body. Her breasts, neck, throat and lips were covered with the soft lips and tongues of three amazing women. Kalina felt herself getting ready to come.

Bettina switched places with Kalina so she could ride her. Kalina got on top and rode Bettina's dick until she got lost in it. Evelyn got behind her and started grinding on her ass the same way she did when they were on the horse together.

Kalina totally surrendered to the pleasure. "Oh God. Fuck me…please don't stop fucking me. Oh God I'm coming….coming so goddamn good."

Kalina shrieked as an orgasm sprang up from the core of her yoni, through her stomach, back down the walls of her pussy, up to her heart. She was screaming and crying, tears pouring down her face. Her EJ sisters were crying too.

After Kalina got hers, they took turns pleasuring each other. Their loving and healing went on all night. When it was done, they were all in the middle of the circle, on the throne of sisterly adoration together, hugging, sobbing and thanking one another.

After they came down from their nirvana just a bit, Regina clapped three times and brought them back to consciousness.

The helpers arrived with bowls of warm milk. Using soft sponges, the helpers cleaned the women with the sweet milk, gave them thick plush towels to dry off with and escorted them one by one to bed.

There were no words spoken or needed for each of them had experienced something that couldn't be expressed in words. *Indulgence. The gift that couldn't be given, only taken.*

Evelyn crawled in the bed and cuddled with Kalina. Kalina welcomed her with open arms.

"I just wanna be clear. I'm not gay, Kalina. But there is something about you that draws me to your spirit."

"I understand, Evelyn. I'm not gay either. I just love...period. Love. Good night, EJ sister. Don't let the bed bugs bite." Kalina said tickling her.

The smell of a gourmet breakfast woke the sisters from their erotic slumber. They showered, packed up and eased toward the smell of yummy omelets, broiled sausage and soy bacon, Belgian waffles, the usual spread of organic fruit, juice and coffee. Chef Stephanie had outdone herself this time.

Regina hugged each of them as they walked into the dining room. She told them how proud of them she was. Kalina was the last one to arrive. Regina kissed her lightly on the lips before she sat down.

Regina clapped three times calling them to order.

"This is our last meal together for this gathering. You all have made powerful progress. I want you to understand that our experiences this weekend are just that. *Experiences.* They don't define us nor are they meant to determine the decisions we make in our future. Your mates and lovers are on the property. They are ready to welcome you home. Not the old you but the new you. After breakfast, we'll do the final exercise of this weekend. Each of you will give what we call, "I will," statements. You will give this statement in the presence of some of the people you love most. I'll go first."

The group stopped eating. This was the first time all weekend that Regina had given them a glimpse into who she was.

"I will treasure this group above all others. I will feed myself your courage and hold fast to the memory of your moment of sheer joy. I will remember how you didn't let fear stop you from experiencing love in its most divine form. Yes, I will."

Kalina wondered what it would be like to re-enter the normal world after an experience like *Erotic Journeys*. Would she be able to find her way back to that life? And more importantly, did she even want to go back?

She turned to Regina. "Regina, can I ask you something?"

"Sure. Anything."

"How do you go back to being normal after something like this? I mean, clearly we can't live this way every day. This....this was one of the most incredible experiences of my life. I healed in ways that I never thought was possible. I discovered wounds I didn't even know existed. What do I do with this—with these experiences? Where do I go from here?"

Regina finishing chewing her eggs and took a sip of OJ before responding. "Pass it on. If and when you meet other women or men who need this medicine, tell them about *Erotic Journeys.*"

"We also have conference calls where you can dialogue with EJ sisters from your class. And of course, as you know, Mahkta offers classes for those who feel called to do this sacred work in deeper ways."

"Thanks, Regina. Thank you for helping us do our work."

Regina smiled, patted her on the hand and flitted away like the butterfly she was.

The sisters grooved their way over to the Great Room for the closing ceremony and to greet their loved ones. An hour later, almost all of them had recited their *I Will* statements and once again, Kalina was the last one to talk.

She knew Regina wasn't going to let her out of it. "Kalina, I believe it's your turn."

Kalina felt Merrill watching her like a hawk. He could see that there was something different about her. She knew what it was. She was free. As free as a bird and ready to take flight.

"I will not take on other people's pain. I will honor and celebrate my body to the fullest. I will not feel guilty or ashamed of my desires. I will always remember I am part of a family of women who practice Nyasa. Yes, I will."

The group cheered for her.

After they said their goodbyes, each woman received a fabulous gift bag with thousands in high-end gift cards and hotel vouchers. They also got a special gift bag stuffed full with groundbreaking sex toys from Evelyn's *Love Pleasures* company and an advance copy of Bettina's new book, *Stupid Crazy Sexy Body*.

On the way home Merrill waited for her to tell him something about what happened at the *Journeys Mansion* but Kalina's mouth stayed closed tighter than a bank vault.

"You gonna tell me what happened or what?"

"I can't talk about what happened with the other women. And my experience was...let's just say it was nothing like I thought it would be and much more than I ever expected."

"You know that doesn't tell me a lot right?"

She tried to summon some of the courage she'd learned at *Erotic Journeys*. "Okay, I confess. Mahkta was right. I was still hurt over something that happened in my childhood. Something I never told you about. When I was thirteen, I came home and caught my father in bed with another woman. He begged me not to tell my mother."

"He said it would destroy her. I kept his confidence but paid a serious price for my silence. I stopped trusting men from that day on."

"Now I understand why you've always been a little insecure in our marriage."

"What's important is that I'm free now. I've forgiven my father and moved on."

"Do you trust me, Kalina?"

"I trust you with my entire soul, Merrill. Not because you can't do wrong but because even if you do, I know I'm strong enough to survive it."

"Have I ever told you how much I love you? How much I admire your strength and worship your power?"

"What are you trying to work up on, Mr. Santiago?" She said laughing.

"Well, it *has* been forty-eight hours since you gave me some."

"Pull this car over then. I got a little something for you. In fact, I think we need to plan our very own *sleepover.*"

"What are *you* trying work up on, Mrs. Santiago?"

"No fear. No shame. Isn't that what Mahkta teaches us?"

"Come on over here and show me." Merrill said pulling over and parking the car alongside the ocean shore....

The Dark Angel By Ifalade Ta'Shia Asanti

Dedicated To My Beloved Pepper

Strength. Through every bow-tie sporting, pointed-toe shoe wearing, blood-sucking lover in a wanna-be stud's suit, she'd clung to it. Guarded it like a ten-carat diamond in a coal-baked mine. Tamala's strength was a black and gold rainbow of justice, a talisman that protected her like a Jesus cross. And like an anchor, it grounded her. Like a net it caught her. When her heart was shattered—broken into a million tiny pieces—it was strength that made her say, "You will not break me! I will survive!"

It was strength that had helped her overcome the Twiggy complex and the urge to wear those Barbie Doll hairstyles. Now she wore her hair as big and nappy as she could get it. And she didn't give a damn when people stared in awe at her Amazon frame and big and round spinning behind.

Tamala slung all one hundred and eighty-five pounds of her stacked body down the rain-washed street. She was music in motion, her rhythm like the dancing flame of a candle with the rush of sweat dripping its wax across her brow. Nobody knew she was jabbing, punching and kicking with each swing and dip of her solid hips. No one knew Tamala was a lavender soldier in a nameless and faceless war. That she was at war with herself and something or someone she called *the divine*.

And now, just when she was moving shit in her life, like a damn near forty year old woman was supposed to, *Max arrived*---leather clad, in a black felt Stetson Brim tipped slightly to the side.

From the counter of *Stella Rue's Coffeehouse*, Tamala watched Max ease out of a blood-red, 1964 Thunderbird, the model with the diamond-shaped back window and tail lights straight out of a Batman movie. Thick silver links around her neck, wrists and fingers gleamed like mercury in a glass thermometer. But even a thermometer couldn't measure the length and depth of the iceberg sleeping in those cold black eyes.

A chill slithered across Tamala's shoulders when Max looked up and over her head, avoiding direct eye contact. How fitting, Tamala thought, as she evaluated Max's stance. Ice for the dirt she'd mentally put over her heart after her ex-lover Michelle had tap danced in her bed.

Tamala was officially a *bitter bitch* living in a reality that refused to be altered by a woman again. But Max......Max wore black like church women wore pastel. It was a statement. A glimpse of the water you were daring to swim in if you chose to venture close. And Miss Tamala was ready to dive.

Tamala decided that Max was a dark energy, almost Gothic. But Black women didn't do Gothic—they were just evil and good at the same time. Tamala wanted some of her evil ass, even if it killed her.

136

Did she dare to try and find some softness beneath the veil of steel once again? And could she recover if things took a turn for the worst? That was the goddamned question!

Max sat down under the glowing orange-yellow lights in Stella Rue's. Vicki, Stella's night waitress, delivered a steaming cup of Latte to her table. Max tossed a ten spot onto her tray. When Vicki tried to give her change back, Max put a flat palm up to her face. Vicki thanked her for her generosity. Max didn't answer, just waved her off with the flick of her hand.

Max didn't verbally invite Tamala over. But her lips and eyes sent the message when they fixed themselves on the empty chair across from where she was sitting. Max tapped the toe of her big leather boot under the table like she was getting tired of waiting for Tamala to bring her ass over. Finally, Tamala got up, walked over and sat down across from her.

"So who are you?" Max asked, in a raspy voice that damn near made her climax when she heard it.

"All things. I am all things." Tamala told her, challenging her hardness with soft but powerful female energy.

Max met the challenge by leaning back in the wrought iron chair and slowly, hypnotically, spreading her legs. She spun her spoon around in her coffee cup until the mocha liquid spilled over the sides onto the saucer.

Tamala felt her armpits start to perspire.

"All things are you, huh? Well it's Max here. Since you're all things, it's nice to meet you Jesus."

"That's Tamala Jesus to you brothah."

Max found that funny. She laughed loudly, not at all shaken by the stares from looky-loos in the coffeehouse. Tamala laughed too.

Tamala realized she hadn't laughed in a really long time. It felt good to let her tummy rumble, to flirt with potential danger again and open her soul just a little.

"Tamala, would you like to go to a concert with me tomorrow night?"

"I might." She answered, feeling like she was peeking over the edge of a looming cliff.

"Tracy's playing at the Strand. I like her, you know. She refuses to be defined and I dig people like that."

The first glimpse into Max's hurricane of a mind somewhat frightened her. She realized Max was trying to let her know she was human, trying to let her in on how she thought.

"Self-definition is definitely the sign of a secure person. Yeah, Max. I'd like to accompany you to check out T.C." She said abbreviating the name of the singer and guitarist, Tracy Chapman.

"Cool. I'll pick you up here at seven. I gotta run.
I'm late for work. Be well Tamala Jesus." She said, rising to
leave.

Tamala wasn't sure if she should just sit there until
Max had gone or get up and leave too. She stayed put until
the Ice Queen was out of the door.

"The bitch didn't even give me her phone number
nor did she ask for mine." Tamala told Vickie, *Stella's
Coffeehouse'* lone waitress.

"Yeah, girl. That was some confidence. Or faith, as
Christian folk call it. So you going out with her or what?"
Vicki said popping her gum and flipping the blonde mop she
called hair.

"You better believe it. I'll be standing in that door
with the clock strikes seven tomorrow night. Death couldn't
keep me from it."

Tomorrow rolled around like the clock was on speed. At six-thirty, Tamala was in the mirror applying lipstick and surveying her attire.

She'd selected the piece of red clothing she owned for their first date. A hip-hugging leather dress with spaghetti straps. She bought a pair of second-hand red sandals to go with it. Her Mother's ruby earrings set the ensemble on fire.

Max appeared in the door of Stella's at seven on the nose. Her expression Tamala she was pleased with what she saw. Tamala knew this because Max flipped her smooth stroll to a mean pimp walk over to her table. Tamala didn't budge until she was standing over her.

Max politely slid her chair back and escorted her out to her car where the Isley Brothers were crooning their hit *In Between the Sheets* from an eight-track player that was still in mint condition. Max reached over and fastened Tamala's seatbelt. Dragged her breasts across Tamala body on the way back to her side of the car.

Max put the car in drive then stamped her foot on the brakes just before they pulled out. She poked her brown fingers into the bottom of Tamala's chin and gently turned her face toward hers.

Max kissed her. Not a tongue kiss, but a searing smear of the lips that made Tamala's heart race. Then, without a word, Max backed out of the driveway and took off.

When they drove into the parking structure Max opened her glove compartment and took a large black gun from beneath the seat. She stuck it in the glove for safe keeping.

Seeing the shock on Tamala's face, Max tried to explain the reason she carried a deadly weapon in her car.

"I work downtown. I get off work at three o'clock in the morning. It's them or me and it damn sure ain't gonna be me, if you know what I mean."

Tamala nodded her head and reached for the door. Max she stopped her.

"Wait right there. I'll be around to get you."

An old school sistah. Tamala loved it. She waited like a good little femme until Max opened the door and helped her out.

The concert was slamming. Tamala saw Max really smile for the first time since they'd met. When Tracy sung her hit song, *Give Me One Reason*, the crowd went nuts. Tamala loved that song. She'd put it on her answering machine's outgoing message when Michelle screwed up.

The evening was incredible. They had such a fabulous time that Tamala hated to see it come to an end.

They went over Max's place for drinks after the show. Max lived in a huge loft in one of the old commercial buildings in Downtown Los Angeles.

There was red, purple and black everywhere she looked. A row of cherry lights were strung above her king-

143

sized, purple comforter wearing bed. Max lit a series of strawberry scented candles in an area she'd sectioned off as the living room. She picked up a remote control, clicked it twice and the melancholy sound of Miles Davis on horn filtered into the room. Tamala kicked off her pumps and relaxed on an onyx leather couch. A few minutes later, Max brought her class of *Ame*, a fruit and herb infused drink from England.

"What do you do for a living, Max?" Tamala braved.

"I answer the phone."

"What, you do phone sex or something?"

"Now that's funny. Wish I could. Don't have the voice for it. Nope. I'm more like an operator. I manage the switchboard for L.A's *Emergency Response Network.*"

"I see. I'm a teacher. I teach art at L.A. City College."

"An art buff, huh? Tell me what you think of this." She said getting a book from the shelf.

It was a collection of photographs featuring body piercings. Tamala quietly flipped through the pages of book. The photos were very well done.

The lighting and angles all heightened the impact of the content. When she got to the end of the piercing book, Max pulled up the white tank top she had on under her black leather jacket.

"I have a total of three." She said, pointing to the two rings in her nipples. Her large, plum nipples made a drop of saliva drip from the corner of Tamala's mouth.

"The other one is in my tongue." She confessed, poking out her tongue.
"Nice. Did it bleed much?"

Tamala's armpits were getting sweaty and that wasn't only part of her getting a little wet.

"It bled for about a week. That's rare. But I have a special tongue." She joked,
flicking it back and forth.

145

Tamala decided Max was a wicked teaser. She figured she better get her shit and get out of there before she ended up giving it to her on their first date.

"Well thank you for a lovely evening, Max."

"It's that time? Come here for a minute before we go." Max said, pointing to her lap.

Tamala swallowed hard and made her way across the room to answer Max's invitation.

"Come on. Come to Daddy." Max said, patting her knees.

Tamala told herself life was too short to miss out on opportunities. So she slid onto her lap and exposed just a tad of her black lace garter and thigh high stockings.

She wrapped her right arm around Max's shoulder and planted light kisses across her face and down her neck. Max's soft lips found their way to Tamala's. Their tongues danced the salsa for a good ten minutes.

Tamala cracked her legs open a little more. Let Max feather her fingers across the pearl. Max kissed and sucked her neck just enough to make Tamala boil inside. She opened her legs a little wider.

Max slid her middle finger inside, slowly slid it in and out. She rubbed, squeezed and teased Tamala's pearl with the other hand.

Tamala met each of her thrusts with a fiery passion. Let her add two, three, four fingers to mix. Max made love to her just like that until an explosive orgasm rocked her so hard she almost fell off her lap.

Max knew she'd gotten her. She took back her fingers, smiled at her victory and rubbed Tamala's juices in between her palms like lotion.

"You're a bad ass." Tamala told her. "I better go home. It's getting late."

"Come and go kind of girl?" Max teased, patting her on the ass to get up.

Tamala smoothed down her dress. Felt the steam between her legs becoming a trickle. She squeezed her legs together to conceal the throbbing that was still ravaging her body.

Max met her at the door with the car keys jingling. They let their souls kiss for the second time that evening.

Tamala fell back against the cement wall behind the front door. Max pinned her against it and slid her tongue deep into Tamala's mouth.

Tamala lifted her leg and wrapped it around Max's ass. Max hiked up the other one and before she knew it, Max was grinding her against the wall fully dressed.

Max held Tamala up with one arm and slid her pants down with the other. When her swollen pearl crushed into Tamala's, Tamala lost all her cool.

Max rode her hard and long until her breathing became shallow. When Max came she roared out her pleasure like a lion in the forest.

"Come with me, Tamala. Give it to me. Come on, baby. Ahhhhhhh!"

"Oh God. Max…. You need to stop….don't stop. Oh God…I'm fucking coming again."

Tamala was barely able to walk when Max was done. Max was still moving like the energizer bunny. She led her to the bedroom, removed the rest of Tamala's clothes and got strapped up.

Max took her like only an authentic butch could and would—on her hands and knees. Tamala let her have every ounce of her love. She screamed, ripped the sheets off the bed and collapsed onto the nectar-soaked sheets when Max made her come a third and final time.

They slept for a while until Max gently shook her awake. "It's three a.m. Should I take you to get some clothes love?"

"I have to work in the morning. A few hours of sleep will do me just fine."

Max beckoned her with a single finger, the same finger that had earned her admission to the magical cave the night before.

"Come have a cup of java with me before we go. I need to wake up so I can drive."

Tamala could smell it brewing and hear it perking.

"Smells good. What flavor is it?"

"My own combination. Hazelnut, vanilla and cinnamon.

When the coffee finished brewing, Max poured her a steaming cupful and spooned a few drops of maple syrup inside. She sat down across from Tamala with a deck of cards in her hand.

"Is it okay if I give you a reading?"

Tamala was feeling adventurous. "Sure. Why not? Go for it."

Max spread out five Tarot cards in a straight line and proceeded to tell Tamala about her past, present and their future based on the cards on the table.

"There was a woman in your life. She left without explanation. You were almost destroyed."

Tamala nodded in agreement. She knew the cards were talking about Michelle, her ex-lover.

"There's a woman who lives far away. She's your savior. She's saved you more than once, in fact, she saved you many times."

"That's my mother."

"Your totem animal is the turtle. His medicine taught you to take your time. That's good. You'll always get where you're going in divine time anyway."

Max took a sip of coffee and continued.

"Even though your heart has been broken, no......shattered, you still believe in love. It, love that is, is

151

knocking at your door again. You want it more than anything. But you're not willing to give up you to have it."

"How'd you know all that?! Are you willing to switch those cards around and tell your own story?" Tamala asked, swallowing a mouthful of Max's tasty coffee.

"Sure. I'm not afraid of what the Gods have to tell me."

Max shuffled the cards several times, cut them in half and spread out five cards for herself.

Tamala's mouth dropped open when all of the same cards from her reading, with the exception of one, were laid out on the table.

There was a man in a black coat with a skeleton for a face standing on a corner in one card. A woman holding the earth in her hands on another. A turtle crossing the road on the third and a heart with drops of blood dripping from it on the fourth. The final card pictured a flamboyant woman dressed in pink. She was holding a small bouquet of flowers while dancing around a perfect heart.

"That's you with the flowers." Max told her smiling. "I'm the heart."

An hour later, they pulled up in front of Tamala's house. Max pecked her on the cheek, got out and opened the door. Tamala jotted her phone number down on a cocktail napkin from the concert and stuck in Max's hand.

Max folded the napkin up and stuck in her ashtray. Tamala didn't ask if she would call and Max didn't promise to. Tamala decided to let it go. Max called her at seven-thirty that morning.

"I didn't want you to be late for work," was her excuse for calling.

"Thanks for waking me up. I almost overslept."

"No problem. How about letting me cook dinner for you tonight."

"Sure. But don't start spoiling me."

"I'll do what I want and you'll let me." Max threw back like a guillotine from her mouth.

Tamala found herself getting turned on.

"I'll see you around six-thirty, Max. Have a good day."

"Peace Miss Tamala Woods." Max said using her real last name for the first time.

Then it hit her. How in the hell had Max known what her last name was? She was sure she never told her. Tamala wondered if the woman was psychic too?

As Tamala was leaving work she noticed a letter in her in-box. A single red rose bud lay on top. When she opened it, she couldn't believe what was written on the inside.

Dear Tamala:

Don't ask me how I know, I just do. I know that we've both been drained by the bullshit people call love. And that I, like you, have no time or room for games. I was looking for you the night I came to

Stella's coffee house. For YOU. Don't be fooled by my sometimes harsh words and cold appearance. I am silk and blackberries waiting for you to stroke and taste my mind. I need to be honored, praised and put in check when necessary. I am ready to bleed for you, a little at a time. I'm a butch so don't be playing me like a punk. Treat me like fine wine and drink me slowly. I have prepared a life for you. Are you hungry for the divine? Max

The battle with the divine was finally over. And destiny was her friend after all. Tamala did ninety-five miles an hour down the 405 with nothing but Max's fingers on her mind.

Fluid Wisdom
Secrets in a loveship create the opening for fear, resentment and contempt. There are some secrets that are best shared with an empathetic ear. However, most heart thoughts are meant for the ears and spirit of they who love you the deepest. True intimacy requires vulnerability. Vulnerability is the very fabric of authentic love. Remember always, in love, be Fluid....

Swan-Tiffany Maxwell-Ifalade

TaShia Asanti

In the presence of their business constituents Fela called her Olivia. When it was just the two of them, he called her *Swan*. The smooth curves of her thick body—the way her hips melted into her thighs—all reminded him of that sleek migratory bird from the Northern Hemisphere.

Fela met Olivia on a yachting expedition with one of his yuppy friends. He expected her to be stuck up and snobby like the rest of the trust fund babies aboard the *Mindful Tyrant.* Instead he found her to be adventurous and earthy with a mind that bordered on genius. As an added bonus, she had a ferocious sexual appetite much like his own.

A few years after they met, Fela and Olivia joined forces to launch *Rave,* a multi-million dollar company that produced social events for the rich and famous. Fela and Olivia's parties quickly became the hottest ticket in

157

Hollywood. Their coveted guest list always included a few A-list celebrities along with the who's who of the financial world.

Business was good and the cash was flowing until Fela's sexual indiscretions threatened to destroy their budding empire. Olivia, the thirty-year old daughter of a wealthy software developer, didn't care if *Rave* went down. She hadn't gotten in it for the cash. She'd helped start *Rave* so she could be around the man she loved and worshipped.

Fela could care less about love. He'd never felt anything like what he thought was just an antique four-letter word for any woman. As far as he was concerned, women were on the earth for one purpose, to bring him pleasure. But he had to admit, there was *something* about Olivia that moved him. Whatever that something was, he intended to keep a wide wall between it and him.

Fela had no problem giving Olivia anything she wanted except, of course, what she desired most—his heart. Since *it* wasn't available, he gave her his body, a body he felt was worth every sleepless night it caused. While Fela's magnificent body had been enough for Olivia he knew the time was coming when she'd demand more. Women always wanted more.

Olivia's mother, who had lived in England with her female partner since Olivia was a small child, taught her that a woman's body was meant to be praised and pleasured by the man she loved. Problem was Olivia had daddy issues. Her father, President and CEO of *Rivers Technology,* had been MIA since the day she was born.

With both of her parents out of the picture, Olivia had grown up in the care of Mimi, her French nanny and a host of service staff who worked at her father's estate. It had been Mimi who taught Olivia self-confidence. Mimi also gave her the quick wit that made her a hit in the business world. Under Mimi's care, she'd grown into an intelligent, self-assured young woman who was slightly desperate for love.

Fela had witnessed the destruction love could cause when his beautiful mother was nearly killed by his father during one of his alcoholic rages. Fela got his father to move out after that but not before he took away the thing his Mother loved most. *Her beloved son.*

Fela's father forced him to work for one of his constituents, a man that peddled drugs to teenagers in the poorest neighborhoods in England. He took him to live at a compound where Fela witnessed unspeakable atrocities that still gave him nightmares.

When he turned sixteen, Fela's mother remarried. A month later, with tears in her eyes, she told her new husband about what Fela's father had done.

Outraged, he hired a detective to find and rescue Fela from the compound. To keep Fela's Father from finding out who helped him escape, they smuggled him out of England and sent him to America.

Afraid of being found, Fela changed his last name from Msola to Wellington. He also shed his British accent, trained until his body was as hard as steel and enrolled in an American college. He met Olivia shortly after he graduated.

Fela's childhood had been a nightmare, a nightmare he'd been running from for a very long time. And no one, not even Olivia, knew he was on the run. Fela worked hard to keep his guards up and his emotions in check so she never would. All he needed was enough money to bring his mother and stepfather to America. He was really close to achieving that goal. A few more *Rave* parties and his Mother would be free forever.

Unfortunately, Fela's untreated emotional wounds got in the way of what could've been a great plan. He acted out the pain from his childhood by having reckless flings with wives of *Rave's* top clients. Olivia took extreme measures to

161

keep Fela from straying with other women. She even started doing side events with a known competitor in their industry.

Olivia had teamed up with Ariel Weathers, a former Vanity model turned event producer. Ariel and Olivia's partnership had the potential to destroy *Rave* but if that's what it took to keep Fela at her side, Olivia was willing to make the sacrifice.

Fela came down hard on her when he found out about her and Ariel working together.

"What the hell were you thinking, Olivia? Ariel just wants our contacts. That's the only thing she doesn't have that we do. What the hell would make you chance Ariel aligning herself with our best accounts?"

Olivia was in the bathroom curling her thick brunette mane. "Maybe if you weren't so busy screwing the wives of our *best accounts*, you'd see that I'm the one getting over. Ariel and I are friends and when she asked me to help her out on a couple of jobs, I did. That's it. End of story."

Fela knew she'd done it to get back at him. Olivia was getting sick of his crap and if he wasn't careful, he'd lose her for good. He reverted to his British-African accent and lured her with sensual words.

"*Oni.* I know what you need, Swan. You need to know that those women mean nothing to me. *Yi ju sibi.* Turn your face to me. You, Olivia, mean everything. Come. Come have a drink with me and let's talk."

Olivia loved it when he spoke to her in his native tongue.

He went to the bar and prepared her favorite sin. Kahlua and milk over ice with a splash of caramel. After feeding her a few sips of the intoxicating fluid, he took her hand and led her to the ceiling-to-floor window that looked out over their downtown Los Angeles penthouse.

"Look at us. We're on top of the world, Aya. No one can take us off our throne. All we have to do is keep the haters away."

163

"You called me Aya. That means wife in your language right? I don't see a ring on my finger." She held out her hand in front of him.

He reached around and slid his hand up her thigh. When she looked back at him, he covered her mouth with his warm, thick lips.

"Fela stop. I…."

"Shhh. Don't talk, Olivia. Feel. Feel me."

He slid his hand up a few more inches until he reached the silky fabric of her black thong. He slipped his hand beneath the material, ran his fingers over her pearl. Gently squeezed and rolled it until she let out a soft moan.

She turned around to face him. After a long, deep kiss, he put her back against the window, dropped to his knees, put one of her legs over his shoulder and continued his work. She pushed herself into his lips, gave him full entry to the passion inside.

Her breath became shallow and airy, a sign that Fela almost had her where he wanted her. He sucked and licked her pearl some more while moving his middle finger in and out of her in an ocean-like motion.

"You….bastard. I hate….hate you."

"You love me, Swan. The yoni doesn't lie."

His tongue danced across her flesh while his finger stirred her like pudding. He lapped up her nectar like a cat drinking its milk. When her thighs were drenched in passion, Fela let his pants drop.

He picked her up, wrapped her legs around his back and carried her to the couch. He turned her around, bent her over the back of the couch and let *Big Boy* take her home. Olivia was so wet Fela had to slow down so he wouldn't lose it.

"God, Olivia. Look how wet you are. You like this don't you, Swan?" Fela said while he dipped it in and out of her.

165

"Yes, Fela. I like...like...like it so much.

Ahhhhh....mmmm....yessss."

Olivia's orgasms were the sweetest pleasure Fela had

ever known. Nothing and no one could compare to the

feeling of her tight juicy walls closing in around his love.

When Olivia came, Fela's heart would open just a

little. And to him, a little was too much. A little scared him.

Even a tiny bit of emotion made him vulnerable to the pain

his mother had suffered. He moved his mind back to a place

of full control.

He teased her. Gave her just an inch or two. She

went crazy. Tried to reach back and grab his ass. Force him

to put all of it inside of her.

"Give it to me, Fela! Give me what's mine!"

He slid it in another two inches while massaging her

pearl with his thumb.

"Oh...God. Yes....Oh God. More Fela! More!"

Fela could barely hold it together. Olivia's insides felt like a warm oily bath. He let her have another few inches."

"I want all of it, Fela. I want the *Big Boy* inside of me. Give him to me."

He let his flesh meet the back of Olivia's sweetness. He slapped her ass and rode her until she was screaming his name.

"Fela....I'm coming...coming for you, baby."

He felt her walls tighten around him. He stroked her pearl while he rode her, watched her writhe with pleasure and pain.

Her sex betrayed him, made his legs tremble, his back arch. He planted his feet, pressed his thighs against the couch and tried to hold back until he was sure she was satisfied.

"Come....come for me, Swan. Let it go, baby."

167

He gripped her thick mane of black hair, turned her face toward him so he could witness it hitting her. He knew she wasn't finished

"Oh God, Fela. I'm coming again. I hate...fucking hate you."

Olivia screamed out as a monster orgasm rocked her body. It was so intense that tears poured down her face in the aftermath.

She crumpled onto the couch and squeezed her legs together. "God...Fela...that was so damn good. I'm still throbbing...."

It was a dangerous game he was playing and a lot was at stake. Fela was used to taking risks, risks that usually paid off.

This time he was in real trouble. Trouble that went way beyond Olivia finding out about his questionable background.

Fela had been working both sides of the table. He too had linked up with the one and only Ariel Weathers, the *Tyra Banks* of the party industry. Fela was in deep, way deeper than Olivia could ever know. He had been working as a silent partner in Ariel's new *Sojourner Events Corporation* for months. And that was just the tip of the iceberg of the lies he'd told his beloved Swan.

When they first met Fela told Olivia he was the son of an African king. That back home in Africa, in the country where his Mother and Father were born, he was a Prince. Told her there was a palace, servants—the whole nine yards, waiting on his back at home.

The way he dressed, the swank apartment he lived in, the phat car he drove, made it all believable. That was the mystique that had drawn her to him, that made her drop to her knees forty-eight hours after they met and drain him of every last drop.

Olivia had hidden something from Fela too. What he didn't know was as explosive as a keg of dynamite. The fuse to that dynamite had been lit four months, ten hours and twelve minutes ago. By the time the sun went down on Saturday, that keg was going to blow.

At the base of the dynamite was another secret that had been hidden not by Fela or Olivia but by God himself. This secret topped both their lies and illusive cover-ups.

Fela always reviewed the guest list for Ariel's parties. There was an RSVP that had gotten by him because the guests had changed his last name so he could pull more American business. When Fela had asked Ariel who Xavier Evanston was, she told him rumor had it, Xavier created a technology that could charge cell phones with solar power.

Xavier had been invited by Stan Ackman, one of their regulars, so Fela didn't question his background.

Mistake. *Big mistake.*

Not only was Xavier a man who knew the truth about Fela's background, Xavier was being tracked by the henchmen of a Drug Lord Fela used to work for. Men who wanted to snuff Fela out to make sure he didn't tell the authorities about their bosses' operation.

Fela and Olivia were on the couch, legs and arms entwined. Olivia had dozed off. Her face wore a satisfied expression.

Fela was drained too—their sex always did that too him. He shook her gently so he could free his arm and go to the bathroom.

"Wake up, Swan. Take a shower with me and let's go have steak somewhere chic. Your loving made me hungry."

"I know what'd like to feed you. Just don't have the energy right now."

He chuckled and told her, "Such a freak. One of the many things I love about you. But we have a lot to talk

171

about. Primarily your departure from Ariel Weather's operation."

"Fine. But you're scrubbing my back and I might make you eat it one more time for getting on my nerves."

"You don't have to twist my arm to make love to you."

After their shower and a little more playtime, they dressed in winter whites from head to toe and went to *Morton's,* a jazzy, three-diamond steakhouse with lots of bling and flare.

When he was sure Olivia had ingested a sufficient amount of alcohol to make her sweetly reasonable, Fela told her what was up.

"The Saturday soiree is your last one with Ariel. You cool with that?"

"Whatever, Fela. You act right and I'll stay on this side of the fence."

"Scoot over here next to me."

She slid over until she was right next to him.

He let his manicured hand drift to the edges of her short white skirt. He looked around to make sure no one was watching. When he was sure the coast was clear, he feathered his fingers across her jewels and watched her body come to life.

"Oh God, Fela. You know I love doing it in public places."

He didn't answer. Just slid his middle finger down over it, pushed that button in and out like he was ringing a doorbell and asking for entry.

After a few minutes of him playing with it, his finger started getting slippery. He whispered in her ear while he dipped in and out of it.

"Did you like how I kissed you earlier? How I sucked it between my lips and licked it until it was swollen?"

"Oh God yes. I loved, loved, loved it." The intensity of having sex in a public place made her as hot as fire.

Fela had two fingers inside of her now. He worked the magic button with his thumb. Their sensual act of defiance was turning him on too.

The way he was sitting, it looked like they were deeply engrossed in conversation. No one could see what he was doing with his hand.

Olivia leaned back, lifted her right leg and opened up a little wider. Fela pumped his fingers inside of her, flicked his thumb back and forth over her magic button. Tears poured down her face as she fought to contain the scream rising in her throat.

Olivia whispered, "I'm coming, Fela. Fuck yes! I'm goddamn coming for you."

He felt her walls close in around his fingers. Felt her throb over and over again. When she stopped orgasming and her breath returned to semi-normal, he sat her up straight, smoothed her skirt down and dried his hand on a linen napkin.

Their waiter snuck up on them. Fela tossed his napkin across his lap to cover his rock hard erection.

The weather noticed the flushed tone of Olivia's face. "Would madam like some more water?"

"Yes….yes please. Sparkling with a few slices of lemon."

"Right away, ma'am. And you sir?"

"Nothing. I'm fine."

Fela was throbbing and bobbing inside of his white jeans.

"Want me to take care of you?" Olivia asked him after the waiter left. Her voice was steamy and lush.

"Too risky. Later. On the way home."

"While we're driving or in the parking lot?"

"Either one. Both sound damn good." He said staring at her like he wanted to drink her bathwater.

"We'll end up in jail for indecent exposure."

175

"We'll be out by the morning. That kind of pleasure's worth a night in jail."

They chowed down on steak, Cesar salad and baked potato. Later they sipped dessert wine and munched on exotic cheeses with sweet fruit. There was a jazz band playing. Fela pulled Olivia onto the dance floor and took her for a spin.

Olivia knew she was the envy of every woman in the house. Patrons were toasting them on their way out of the door.

In the parking lot Fela opened Olivia's car door and was heading around to the driver's side when Olivia pulled him to her and kissed him with every bit of her fire.

She turned around, put her ass on his crotch and did a slow, sexy grind until he rose to the occasion.

"Swan...baby...what you doing? You know they have cameras down here."

"Fuck those cameras. If they're watching, let's give them a show."

"We might end up on Youtube."

"I don't care."

"Uh, I do."

"Get in the car then. Thought you were daring. Adventurous. Not afraid of a challenge."

"I am. Just don't wanna end up being the next *Honey Meets Mr. Marcus* video."

"Can't believe I'm damn near begging you to have sex with me."

"You know what…..turn around."

"What?"

"I said, *turn around.*" His voice had an edge to it that made her skin tingle.

She gave him her backside again.

He reached beneath her dress and snatched her thong off with a snap.

"Take it. Take this shit, Fela."

Fela used his index finger to test the temperature of her love. It was hot, baking, ready for him to cook it to perfection.

She reached back and massaged him until he was oven-ready. Unzipped his pants and let it bounce on the back of her ass. She was about to slide him into her when the door that led to the elevators swung open.

Felix pushed her off of him. Olivia yanked her skirt down. Felix turned toward the car and fiddled with the key like he was opening the door.

Fela yanked his shirt down over his bulging erection. The man and his woman walked right toward them. They were about to be exposed.

Right before they reached them, the man and woman got into a car two doors down. Fela and Olivia breathed a sigh of relief.

After he let Olivia in, Fela jogged around to the driver's side. Olivia was cracking up at how close they'd come to being busted.

"You know you're crazy right?" Fela said, chuckling a little bit.

"What would life be without crazy?" Olivia teased.

Inside the car, Olivia's passion took over again. She leaned down, took Big Boy between her lips and slid her mouth up and down him.

"He tastes like candy." She said while slurping him between her lips.

"Shit….slow down, Swan. You're gonna make it pop too fast."

She kept it up until he was hard as a bag of rocks.

Fela leaned back to enjoy the pleasure and the driver door accidentally opened. His left arm went to the ground to keep him from falling out of the car. Olivia still didn't stop working him. Instead, she straddled him, pulled him up and

179

back into the car. She rode him until he exploded like fireworks on the 4th of July.

When they were done, Fela got quiet. He was rarely quiet after sex so Olivia got a little worried.

"Something wrong, baby? You need some more?"

"I'm good. That was…that was amazing."

"What is it then? I can see it on your face. Don't lie to me, Fela.

"I….just want you to know that even though we never made this…us…official, I care about you. I'm just not…ready to settle down. But I want you to know there's no one, no one in this world other than my mother, that I've ever cared about like I do you."

"Fela, where is all this coming from? You act like you're going somewhere. You leaving me or something?"

As much as he wanted to tell her what was going on and why he was working so hard, he couldn't risk involving her. He had to get his mother to safety and then he would figure out his future. Unfortunately, that future didn't include Olivia.

"Think I'm just tired. You actually wore me out for once. Didn't think you had it in you."

"I'm a woman. That means I'm mysterious and unpredictable. Unlike some women, I believe my desires are sacred. The pleasure I give myself is a birthright, a right no one can take from me."

She held up her hand for a high five. He slapped it, stuck the key in the engine and headed toward home.

While they drove he prepped her for the Saturday soiree.

"I want us to shine at Ariel's party. The consummate power couple. Let's wear something that makes us stand out. That black dress you bought during *Fashion Week* in Paris. And those lace up sandals with the fish nets."

"Sounds good. You should wear your tux with the red bow tie and white shirt. Makes you look like a million bucks."

"And you put on that sexy ass fire engine red lipstick that makes you look like you just stepped off the pages of Vogue."

"Done."

"Swan, I have a feeling something big is about to happen. We have to trust the universe that whatever happens is for the best."

"When'd you get so deep, Fela?"

"I'm not trying to be deep, Swan. Just thinking ahead."

At home, Fela and Olivia took a hot shower together, crawled into the bed and slept like the dead.

Mimi, Olivia's childhood nanny and now live-in housekeeper, woke them up the next day around one o'clock.

She knocked lightly on their bedroom door, not sure if she should disturb them.

"Mademoiselle, shall I clean your room? I finished the rest of the house. I should skip it this time, yes?"

Olivia yawned, stretched and glanced at the clock. She looked at the spot next to her and noticed Fela was gone.

"No, I'm getting up. Give me just a few minutes."

Olivia slipped into a cream-colored silk robe, emptied her bladder, splashed cold water on her face and rinsed out her mouth. After fluffing her hair, she went looking for Fela.

Mimi sashayed up to her with a message from Olivia's M.I.A. boyfriend. Her blazing red hair was in a flawless bun. Her lips were painted in the same eye-catching shade.

"Mr. Fela said to tell you he went to the bank. He'll return around two. He is bringing lunch. Indian."

"Thanks, Mimi."

"Madam, I need to tell you something?"

"Mimi, I told you, you don't have to call me Madam anymore. We've been together over twenty years and you're like family. What is it you have to tell me?"

"He…Mr. Fela—he had a lot of things with him when he left."

"Things? What things?"

Olivia darted through the house looking to see what was gone. Mimi was on her heels.

"Clothes, CD's, books. *Things.*"

Olivia realized what she was saying.

"I…I appreciate you letting me know."

"Just one thing I must say to you, Olivia. You deserve the best. Never let a man give you his seconds."

Olivia's eyes teared up for a minute.

"Thank you, Mimi. Thank you for always being present. I want you to take the rest of the day off. In fact, take the rest of the week off. You deserve it. Go do something fun. Go home to Paris. Visit your family. You

184

know where my Amex card is. Treat yourself to whatever. I love you."

Mimi hugged and kissed Olivia on the cheek before gathering her things and heading toward the door. Mimi loved Olivia like she was her own. She'd practically raised her.

On the other side of town, Fela was flirting with a teller at First Mutual Bank. He'd just closed out him and Olivia's business account. Cashier's check in hand, he blew a kiss at the blonde-haired beauty who let him close the account without a second signature.

"Soon. I will see you *very* soon, Amanda."

Amanda blew a kiss back at him and nodded her understanding.

When she was sure Fela was gone, Amanda grabbed the phone and called Olivia. When she hung up, Olivia had the full 411 on the stunt Fela had pulled with their bank account.

Juggling enough Indian food for a small party, Fela called out to Olivia as he walked in the door.

"Olivia! Where are you? I brought lunch. I hope you're ready to go."

Olivia was dressed to the nines. Designer jeans blinged out with pink rhinestones and silver studs, hot pink tank top, Jimmy Choo's on her feet. Her long black hair was down and curled on the ends. It swished across the crest of her full ass.

"Damn, Olivia. Whose all that for?"

"You. Who else would I be getting dressed up for? I'm just kidding. I'm meeting Ariel for lunch. Afterwards we're going to the spa."

"When'd you two become best buddies?"

"It's lunch and a spa date, Fela. Girls do it all the time. It's called female bonding."

"Like I said, when did you two get close enough to spend time bonding?"

186

"*Anyway*. Put my food in the fridge. I'll be hungry when I get back. See you around four. I'll take a power nap and get dressed for the soiree."

"Cool. Keep your cell with you in case I need to get in touch. I'm closing a deal with P. Diddy's peeps for their New Year's Eve bash and I might have a question."

"Always on the mainline for you, Fela."

Olivia decided not to say anything about what Mimi or Amanda told her. Instead she watched and paid close attention.

Her father might not have been there to raise her but one thing he had taught her was how to protect her business. She'd been transferring the profits from *Rave* events into an account Fela knew nothing about for years.

After Olivia left, Fela walked through the house reminiscing on he and Olivia's four years together. He truly regretted ending such a sweet business relationship. Their arrangement was absolutely perfect. He made a shitload of money, got all the sex he wanted and slept with whoever he felt like banging. Maybe, he thought to himself, after things died down he'd reconcile with Olivia and make her Mrs. Fela Wellington…

After working out for a few hours in their state of the art gym, Fela took a refreshing nap. The sky was dark when he woke up. He called out to Olivia to remind her to get dressed.

When she didn't answer, he meandered through the house trying to find her. Figuring she was either downstairs in the gym working out with headphones on or in the steam room relaxing, he took a dip in the Jacuzzi and nursed a glass of fruity vodka. Thirty minutes later, Olivia still hadn't turned up. Fela speed dialed her cell ready to tear into her for being late.

She answered on the first ring. There was a lot of noise behind her.

Fela was a little irritated that Olivia sounded all bubbly, like she was having the time of her life.

"Hey babe. Ariel got invited to a designer gown sale at Barbara Streisand's estate. She got me on the list. You'll never believe who I'm rubbing elbows with. The wives of every major star in Hollywood."

"That's great, Olivia. But we have a party tonight and we need to talk about strategies for pulling new clients. I need you to get your ass home so we can prepare."

"I was getting ready to call you about that. I'm gonna meet you there. I had Mimi bring my clothes. You were asleep so I told her not to wake you."

"That's not gonna work, Olivia. We need to walk in together. I want us to make a grand entrance."

"Fine. I'll have my driver park down the hill until you arrive."

"I guess that'll work. But from here on out, when you change the plans, let me know in advance." Fela said hanging up the phone without a goodbye as a way to let her know he was irritated.

When Olivia hung up, she turned to Ariel and said, "Part two of our plan is in full effect."

A little after nine, Fela rolled through the steel gates of Ariel's magnificent property in his pearl white Lamborghini. Olivia was waiting for him at the bottom of the hill just like they'd planned.

Olivia joined him in the Ghini and they rolled up the hill to make the entrance of all entrances.

As he and Olivia made their way through the maze of A and B lists celebrity guests at Ariel's soiree, Fela kissed the hands of every beautiful woman. Olivia complimented Fela's flirty greeting with the traditional Hollywood air kiss.

Olivia lifted a sparkling glass of champagne from the silver tray of a uniformed server as she passed by. Fela followed suit. He also treated himself to a tapa or two and way too many prawns dipped in lemon and garlic butter.

The bullshit and drinks was flowing from every corner. Everything was going according to plan until Fela and Olivia went out by the pool to take a toke off a Cuban cigar and compare notes.

Ariel and a few of her friends were sitting in a cabana, laughing and drinking. There was a tall, dark, handsome man sitting next to Ariel and a woman in a red dress at the other end of the couch. Olivia recognized the red-dress woman as Candy, Ariel's executive assistant. Ariel beckoned them over to join the group.

When Fela saw the man sitting next to Ariel he stopped dead in his tracks.

Olivia pulled him along. "Come on, Fela. Ariel wants to introduce us to her friend. That's the solar-powered-cell-phone-charger guy I was telling you about."

Fela tried to talk but his tongue locked up on him. When he could finally talk again, all that came out was, "I gotta...gotta go take a pee."

"Not before you meet Ariel's guest. Don't be rude."

Ariel's ash blonde hair was pulled tight into an immaculate chignon. A diamond encrusted choker held center court on her neck. She wore a New York black halter jumpsuit that pimped out her tanned cleavage.

When the handsome man looked up and saw Fela, his face contorted into an expression of disbelief. Fela's expression settled somewhere between shock and outright fear.

Ariel stood, "Xavier Evanston, meet Fela and Olivia of *Rave Inc.* These are the two I was telling you about. If you want the media to attend your product launch, if you want A-list celebrities to show up, this is who should produce the event."

Olivia looked at Fela then shifted her eyes to Ariel's guest.

"Have you two met before?" Ariel asked, as a butler refilled her champagne.

Olivia watched for a sign that he might be lying.

Xavier spoke up first. "No.. ..but he looks exactly like my younger brother who passed away from AIDS last year. It…it's uncanny."

A British accent with an island flavor rolled off Xavier's tongue as he spoke.

Fela gathered himself. "I'm very sorry to hear that. Xavier is it? Good to meet you." Fela stuck out his hand to greet the man.

Xavier turned his attention to Olivia. "Olivia's a nice name. William Shakespeare made it famous. It has German origin yes? You have German ancestry?"

Olivia heard something familiar in his voice.

It hit her like a tree falling in a quiet forest. Xavier's accent sounded just like the one she'd heard Fela use a zillion times in the four years they'd been together. Fela and Xavier had the same geographical inflections on their tongue!

"You're good, Xavier. I was named after my grandmother whose ancestors were taken to Germany during the middle passage. Is that a beautiful West African patois I hear on your tongue?"

Xavier's nervousness was evident but he played it off like a pro. "I grew up in England but my parents were born in Nigeria. It's in the blood for sure. Have you been to Africa?"

"Not yet. But it's on my list of destinations. Perhaps you could escort us."

"I don't know the land well enough to take you on a proper tour. But I could certainly connect you with a tour guide who does."

Olivia let the conversation drop. Fela was as a quiet as Pacquiao after that historic knock-out by Marquez.

Ariel saw it too. The familiarity in Fela and Xavier's eyes. Ariel called Olivia to the side to confer with her.

"Olivia, can I steal you away for a minute? I need to go over some details for an upcoming event with you. And Candy, I need you to help Olivia and I find something. The bartender just texted me that we're out of Cognac but I'm sure I saw two full cases of it in the wine cellar. We'll be right back gentleman. Please order anything you like. And I do mean anything."

Inside, Ariel grabbed Olivia's hand and led her through the living room, around the now packed house, to her personal office. Ariel's office was huge, the size of a small apartment. To the left of her desk was a wall with twelve miniature TV's. Ariel picked up a remote control and zeroed in on one in particular.

"I think Xavier and Fela know each other. I don't know how but we can find out if you want to."

Olivia went into protection mode. She still felt loyal to Fela even though he betrayed her. She hated what love did. She wished she could drill it out like a cavity.

"How can you find out?"

"The entire house is on live stream video. I did it for security purposes and because my insurance policy requires it but I also use it to get the upper hand on my clients. We can listen to their conversation right now if you want."

"I'm not sure I want to know."

"You *need* to know who Fela really is. Stop being weak and codependent and be the empowered woman I know you are."

"Whatever."

"Is that a yes?"

"I said, *whatever.* Sure, turn up the volume and zoom on in."

When Ariel zoomed in, Olivia was shocked to see Fela crying. In the four years they'd been together, she'd never seen him cry.

"Turn it up. I can't hear them." Olivia told her.

When she heard the pain in Fela's voice, she immediately felt guilty for listening in.

"Staying away from you and Mom has been the hardest thing I've ever had to do. I knew those men would kill me or kill you and mom if I came back. I've got the money now. I can get you two out of there for good. I know people that can change our names and get us new passports. We'll have a good life here in America."

Xavier fought to maintain his composure.

"Son, I've been trying to contact you for months. All of your old numbers are disconnected. The emails I send you bounce back. Your Mother is here already. I have her in a safe house in San Francisco. Your sister's there too."

197

Olivia's hands flew up like she was under arrest. "Oh my God. That's Fela's father!"

Ariel was unmoved by Fela's emotions. She knew something Olivia didn't.

"That can't be his father. Not if he's reacting like that. Fela hates his father. He was an animal—a raging alcoholic who nearly beat his mother to death. She must've remarried. That has to be Fela's stepfather."

Olivia was shocked. "Fela told you that? He spoke to you about his past? I mean, I knew you two were working together but...."

"Let me be up front with you. I slept him when we first connected. I had too. He wouldn't have trusted me otherwise."

"I had a feeling you did. But I wasn't sure."

"That was business. It meant nothing to me. I love *you*, Olivia. I love you like Fela never has, will or could."

"I love you too, Ariel. I love both of you. I want to be your wife. I wanted Fela to be my husband. I want to have babies that the three of us could raise together."

"We'll have our children. We'll be chic lesbians roller blading down Santa Monica with our babies in state-of-the-art strollers. I have the best Vitro guy in the country on speed dial. We don't need Fela's misogynistic sperm."

Ariel leaned over and kissed her. Stuck her soft tongue so far down Olivia throat she almost choked. She rolled Olivia's nipple between her finger tips and made her pearl jump to life. Olivia kissed her back with the same amount of fire and passion.

"I'm sorry he lied to you, Mademoiselle."

"Stop talking and make love to me. I need sex to get me through this." Olivia told her.

Ariel took Olivia's breast in her mouth. Flicked her tongue back and forth against her juicy nipple. Sucked it hard then soft then hard again until Olivia was whimpering. Olivia

199

kissed Ariel's neck, bit her just a little then sucked until a small red mark appeared. She knew how much light pain turned Ariel on. They would've gone at it, torn each other's clothes off and did the do right there if a loud knock hadn't pulled them out of it.

It was security.

"Ma'am, I'm sorry to bother you but there's a problem out by the pool."

Ariel turned the volume back up and zoomed the camera in again.

Three burly men were forcibly escorting Fela and his Stepfather out the back gate.

"Oh my God! Get out there and help him!" Olivia shouted.

"Sorry but I only take orders from Ariel." The guard said.

Ariel gave them a command. "Do what you can to keep them from taking Fela and his father. But I cannot have a scene. No one can know what's going on. Understood?"

"Yes ma'am."

The security guards took the side entrance and cut off the goons. The men scurried their hostages back to the pool area and searched for an alternative exit. The guards closed the front entrance so the men couldn't drive off the property.

Olivia watched in horror as Xavier snatched the gun out of the holster of one of the goons. He shot his two cohorts and attempted to kill the third man but he wasn't quick enough.

The third man fired on Xavier. Xavier dove behind the bushes. Then the man turned the gun on Fela.

Olivia gasped and screamed, "Run Fela! Run!"

"He can't hear you, Olivia. Calm down. My men are there now." Ariel told her.

Ariel's guard tasered the third man. Shot a bolt of electricity into him that sent him to his knees. The music and partying was so loud, the guests didn't hear a thing.

In what seemed like minutes, the guards moved the bodies of the shot and tasered men into a sequestered area and got Xavier into a car to the hospital. They hosed down the area and straightened things up before anybody came out.

"I need to go to him." Olivia told Ariel in tears.

"You need to wait a few minutes. My men are making sure there's no more of those goons on the property."

After a few minutes went by Ariel told her, "I can't believe you. He went behind your back and partnered up with your competitor. He took money out of your account and was ready to leave you high and dry. Tonight you found out he's been lying about who he is. Lying to your face for years. Yet you still care for him."

"He did it for his mother. And that, in my opinion, is honorable. I've lied to him too. I love you, Ariel. I'm *in love* with you. But you knew who I was when we started seeing each other. Look, I need to go see about Fela."

Olivia hurried through the living room, around the tennis courts and out to the pool. Fela was sitting on a lawn chair. His eyes were filled with tears. He was heaving, throwing up from the trauma of what he'd just gone through.

He wiped his mouth on the back of his hand. Olivia handed him a bottle of water and grabbed a towel off the chair for him to clean his face. She wondered if Ariel was watching them on the close circuit cameras.

"Olivia, I'm so sorry. Sorry I lied to you. Sorry I held back my feelings...I shut down because I knew I had to leave. My mother. They were going to kill her. I had to get her out of there. I had to survive until I could."

"Shhhh. Be quiet now, Fela. I know enough to understand why you did what you did. What I don't know, you'll tell me in due time."

He reached in his pocket and pulled out the cashier's check.

"I want you to redeposit this tomorrow. I took the money out of the business account. Thought I needed it to get my mother to America. Xavier is….Xavier is my stepfather. He's the only real father I've ever known. He saved me when I was a kid. And now I'm the reason he might die."

"Don't project, Fela. What hospital did they take him too?"

"They said he was going to a private hospital. It all happened so fast. We looked up and my father's men were telling us to shut up and follow them. After it was over, Ariel's security cleaned everything up so fast."

"I saw it all on the camera in Ariel's office."

"What? She has cameras out here?"

He looked around for the cameras. "It doesn't matter. I don't even care anymore. Look, there's something else I have to tell you. I've been working with Ariel for three months. I needed the money. Or should I say I needed money you couldn't track."

"I know, Fela. I know who you are."

"I don't think you do. Those women I slept with— they meant nothing to me. Just a way to stay disconnected from my emotions."

She chose her next words carefully.

"It's all over now. You need to figure out what you want to do with your life now that you and your family are free."

"I already know what I want to do with my life. I love you, Olivia. I've never loved any woman except my mother. But I know without a shadow of a doubt that I love you. You were all I thought about when the men pulled their

205

guns out. If you can ever find it in your heart to forgive me for being a low-life hustler, liar, cheater and thief, I'll try my best to show you the man I can be."

"I can't promise anything right now. What I can say is I'm open. Are you open, Fela?"

"What do you mean?"

"There's something I need to tell you too."

They heard someone walking up behind them.

"What she needs to tell you is not only have we been fucking for the last few months, she's my woman. And if you ever do anything that jeopardizes her safety or hurts her heart again, I will personally kick your ass and put a bullet between your eyes. You understand me, Fela? Capesh?" Ariel said with a smirk of a smile.

"What? What is she talking about, Olivia?"

"Ariel and I are….together. I love her, Fela. All those nights you were out screwing other women behind my back. It was Ariel that wiped my tears and comforted me."

206

"Apparently she did a little more than comfort you." He looked over at Ariel. "Guess you're the clean-up woman in reverse. You two double-crossed me."

"No, *you're* the clean-up man. And yes, you're the victim of a master rope-a-dope my friend. And I hate to tell you this right now, but you're also fired."

"Whatever. I don't care about working for you. I never did."

He turned his attention to Olivia.

"So you knew about me taking the money out of the bank?"

"That woman you flirted with at the bank—she's Ariel's cousin."

"Damn, that bitch has eyes everywhere. Let me tell you right now—I don't do triangles. You can have your fling if you want. When you're ready to have a family, when you want a real relationship, you know where to find me." Fela said, trying to redeem his manhood a little.

207

"Really? Really, Fela? You're mad at me now?" Olivia asked him.

"I told you I wasn't ready to settle down. I never said we were exclusive. Not once."

"That's true. But out of the same mouth you forbade me to see other men."

Fela was quiet for a few minutes. When he spoke, he shocked everybody.

"You're absolutely right, Olivia. You didn't deserve to be treated the way I treated you. You're a queen and I treated you like a bitch. I'm lucky you even want to talk to me."

He walked over to her, took her hand in his. "After I go to the hospital and see my father and fly to San Francisco to see my mother for the first time in four years, I want us to talk. I'm willing....I'm willing to do whatever it takes to have you in my life. Even if that means accepting you and....Cruella. If you'll accept me that is."

Ariel stood up. "At least your punk ass has a little honor. Olivia, I'm gonna go tend to my guests. Handle your business. I'll see you later tonight?"

"Yes. I'll be back."

Ariel kissed Olivia before leaving. Kissed her deep enough for Fela to know their relationship was way more than a fling.

When Ariel was gone Fela made a request of Olivia.

"If you're not too busy or too angry at me, would you mind coming with me to the hospital to see about my father?"

"I'll go with you. Let me get my coat."

***

Turned out the bullet that hit Fela's father went through the flesh of his right shoulder. Minor surgery was all he needed. That, some good pain meds and a few weeks in a sling and he would be fine.

Even though the three men who followed his stepfather had been taken care of for good, Fela had to be sure there weren't others. He waited three weeks before contacting Xavier and his mother.

In those weeks following the shooting at Ariel's mansion, Fela became a different man. When Olivia met him he was a selfish, self-absorbed little boy. Now he was a selfless, incredibly giving man who spoiled Olivia rotten.

He cooked traditional Nigerian dishes for her. Fed her Fufu covered in a delicious red sauce directly from his fingers. He made homemade Italian dishes he learned how to cook from one of his college friends in London. He brought her breakfast in bed.

He showered Olivia with flowers and candy. They explored *Kama Sutra* poses designed to increase emotional closeness. Their sexual relationship went to a whole new level. Now he made love to Olivia instead of screwing her.

Fela thought Olivia would get over Ariel and date him exclusively. But when he and Olivia weren't spending time together, she and Ariel were darn near inseparable. He made a decision to let that go and focus on making the most of the moments she was with him.

Three weeks later, Fela, Xavier and Olivia flew to San Francisco to see Fela's mother. When they arrived at the small, peach-colored stucco house just north of the Golden Gate Bridge, Fela got emotional.

"I'm not sure what to say. It's been so long." Fela told Olivia and Xavier.

"Tell her that. God will take care of the rest." Xavier told him.

"What should I call her? What's her name?" Olivia asked Fela.

"Her name is Safiya. You may call her Miss Safiya."

211

As they walked down the rose bush lined walkway, the front door of the house flew open. Fela's mother came running down the path into her son's arms.

She was a buxom woman with ebony skin as smooth as satin. Her Nubian locked hair was twisted into a sophisticated updo. She wore traditional clothes made from brightly colored African fabric. Seven or eight brass bracelets jingled on her left wrist.

Fela ran to her. "Iya Mi. Is it really you my dear mother?"

"Omo. Come here my son. Let me look at you."

They cried and hugged each other as they walked toward the door.

After they calmed down, Miss Safiya told her son. "To witness my son eating my food...I didn't know if I'd ever get to cook for you again. Olodumare has brought us a mighty long way. But we are together now. And nothing will ever tear us apart."

His mother had cooked a fabulous dinner. Olivia ate so much she thought she would burst. After the tears dried the laughter began. Story after story about family members and friends who Fela hadn't talked to for years.

"So I hear I have a little sister."

"She is asleep in the care of her nanny. You'll meet her in the morning. I knew our first meeting would be emotional and didn't want to frighten her. Her name is Amina. She's four. Xavier and I are very proud."

"I'm sure I will love her."

His mother looked over at Olivia.

"Tell me about this pretty woman you've brought to meet me. Is this your wife?"

Olivia waited for Fela to answer.

"I want her to be. She's a good woman. She's a huge part of why I made it here to be with you tonight."

Miss Safiya took Olivia's hand in hers. "Thank you, daughter. Thank you for caring for my son. I shall be your Mother too. You can call me, Iya."

"Thank you, Iya. It's an honor to finally meet you."

Fela's mother began clearing the table.

"Please, allow me. I was taught that the cook never cleans."

Olivia took the dishes from her and headed toward the kitchen.

After she cleaned up the dishes, she realized it was almost time for them to head back to the airport. "Fela, should I call and reschedule our flight back to Los Angeles?"

"No. We have business in the morning. I will return to San Francisco on Monday. And then our family will make up for lost time."

Xavier got up to walk them to the door. While Olivia said her goodbyes to Miss Safiya, Xavier had a few words with Fela.

"Son, when you get back I want to talk to you about a job with my company. COO. The position is yours if you want it."

"I'm down by law."

"What?"

"It's an American saying. It means I must support you because I love you."

Xavier smiled and told him, "Son, there's something else you should know. Your father was killed yesterday. One of my colleagues in Nigeria called me. It's all over the papers. It's really over. They can't hurt us now."

"Wow. It's weird but I don't feel sad. I hardly feel anything. Maybe a bit relieved. I won't be attending his funeral. It wouldn't be right. But I will pray for his soul to be better in the next life."

Xavier nodded his understanding, shook Fela's hand and patted him on the shoulder. Before he got in the limo, Fela turned around and hugged Xavier.

"You're my dad. The only father I've ever known. Thank you for stepping up and doing what he never did or could."

"I love you, son."

At the airport, Olivia and Fela chilled in the Red Carpet room and sipped Cappuccino. Fela got a text advising him that their flight was delayed for two hours.

Fela had a craving for one of those Cubanos. He still had a couple in his satchel from Ariel's party.

"Olivia, let's take a walk. I need a cigar. And a stiff drink."

"Let's get the drink first."

"Let's."

They ordered Bailey's and coffee from one of the bars in the terminal. When that sweet dark liquor started to warm their bodies and calm their hearts, they took the elevator to the parking lot to puff their Cubanos.

216

Fela lit Olivia's first, then made the tip of his own cigar glow a fiery red.

The smoke was sweet and mellow. They stood by the ashtray, puffed their cigars and unwound.

"Fela, remember that time I wanted you to sex me in the parking lot?"

"Yeah. I thought you were crazy but I was hella turned on."

"Nobody's down here."

"Yeah but you *know* they have cameras at the airport and unlike the ones at the restaurant, you best believe they're watching."

"Let's give them something to look at."

"You're crazy. TSA will lock our asses up."

"Not if they can't prove we were doing anything. It'll be one helluva memory when we're old and gray."

"That mean you're gonna marry me?"

"It depends."

"On?"

"What you do in the next two minutes."

He snuffed out his Cubano, took her hand and walked her down the parking lot toward the stairs. When they were in the staircase, he asked her for some lipstick.

"What for? You can't play with my *Mac* lipstick. It cost a grip and I…"

"I'll buy you some more. Give it to me *now*."

His aggression turned her on. She went in her purse and handed him a tube of red lipstick.

He stood in the stairwell and lit his stoogie. He colored a big red circle on the cocktail napkin his drink came with and walked up two more steps.

"Found it. The camera's blind spot." He stood on his tiptoes and dropped the napkin over the camera.

Fela sat down on the steps and had Olivia stand over him.

"Hold on to the rails and crouch down on my face."

218

"Are you serious?"

"Do it. And don't ask me any more questions."

She slid her dress up to her thighs and did just what he said. When her yoni was over his face, he started kissing it through her panties.

"Ohhhh God."

He slid her panties to the side and took her pearl between his lips. Olivia darn near lost her footing but she held on.

"Fela….Jesus Christ."

He sucked and licked her, sucked and pulled until she was as wet as a thousand rivers.

"That feels….so fucking good. Suck it, Fela. Suck me good."

He twirled his tongue around and on it and took it between his lips. Sucked it like it was a baby bottle until she was nice and juicy. He unzipped his pants and let Big Boy bounce to life. He rubbed it over her pearl, let her feel how hard and strong he was.

"Fela, you're gonna...you're gonna make me come already. Slow it down, baby."

He slid into her. Damn near came himself. Olivia was so hot and wet—he could hardly hold it together.

"We don't....don't have a lot of time. They saw us come in here."

"That's it.....right there. Oh Godddddd."

She started bouncing up and down on him, using the bars to keep her footing. Fela starting moaning too.

"Olivia....slow down, baby. I can't take much more.....ahhhh."

"Do it with me, Fela. Come with me. Come. With. Me!"

Fela starting slapping her ass. He grabbed her hips and pulled her to him again and again.

"I'm coming, baby. Shit.....I can't hold it."

"Yes. Give me that shit, Fela! Come for me!"

Olivia slid down on him so her pearl would rub against the base of his shaft. He was deep inside of her trying to hold out until she got hers. She twirled her hips, slammed her mound into him over and over. When he came he released a beautiful, pleasure-filled moan.

Olivia's orgasm snuck up on her, possessed her entire body. She forgot where she was. Forgot she was on a staircase in an airport terminal. She started screaming like somebody was killing her. She came harder than she ever had. Multiple orgasms ripped through her body like she'd been hit by a freight train.

They were both far too gone to notice the woman who'd walked into the stairwell. She stood at the bottom of the steps watching them with an odd expression on her face.

Fela opened his eyes first. When he saw the woman he pushed Olivia off of him. Caused her to scrape her knee on the cement steps.

"What the fuck are you doing here?"

"Shit, Fela. Look what you made me do!"

Olivia jerked around, still holding her knee, which was now bleeding.

"Ariel. How did….when did….what's going on?"

Olivia's body was still twitching. Fela was rock hard but the fear had him deflating at warp speed.

"I just wanted to see what made you so…so pathetic when it comes to him."

"How did you know where we were?"

"I was on my way back to L.A. from a business trip and saw you and Fela getting on the elevator. I followed you to the parking lot to talk to you but chickened out when I saw you two go into the stairwell. I was leaving until I heard the screams. I came in here to make sure you were okay."

Fela was pissed.

"I think you're stalking us. Look, I don't invade the time you and Olivia spend together and I'd appreciate you staying in your fucking lane when we're doing us."

"Well, you don't have to worry about that anymore. It's over between Olivia and I. I can't handle this. I don't want to go behind a damn man. Don't want to taste you on her lips when I kiss her. Matter of fact, I *hate* the scent of you on her body."

"Ariel, let's talk about this when I get back."

"Nothing to talk about. I saw what I needed to see. I can't compete with that."

Fela zipped up his pants, tucked in his shirt and checked their ticket.

"Swan, let's go. We've gotta get back and catch our flight."

"Congratulations, Fela. You won." Ariel said with tears streaming down her face. She turned around and walked toward the door.

"Ariel, don't do this!"

"Don't do what? I thought I could handle it but I can't. Seeing you screaming like that, him sexing you—it killed something in me. Call me and make arrangements to get your stuff. Take good care of yourself, Olivia. And Fela, don't forget what I told you that night in my backyard."

That made Olivia smile. Ariel had threatened to kill Fela if he hurt her.

"I love you, Ariel. I always want you to know that."

"Sometimes love isn't enough." Ariel said before she turned around and walked out of Olivia's life for good.

Olivia straightened out her skirt, smoothed her hair down and refreshed her lipstick. Just as they were heading toward the door, it flung open again.

This time it was TSA.

"Our computers registered a lot of activity in this corridor. What's going on?"

Fela told him. "We just needed a smoke."

"This is a no smoking area. You can smoke over there by the elevators where the ash-rays are."

"No problem, officer."

They walked toward the elevator with huge smiles on their faces. When they were out of TSA's earshot, they fell out laughing.

"That story should be in a book." Fela said as they made their way back through security.

"Definitely going down as one of freakiest places we made love."

When they were back in the terminal, back in the *Red Carpet* room, Fela went in his carry-on bag and pulled out a small black box.

"I was planning on doing this when we got home to L.A. but after what just happened, I think I've earned the right to at least ask."

He opened the box, went down on one knee and took her hand in his. Eyes darted in their direction. A couple of men smiled and a few women looked envious.

"You loved me when you had no idea who I was. And after you found out, you still loved me. Olivia Rivers, would you give me the honor of being my wife."

She tried to control it but the tears started flowing.

"Yes, Fela, I will be your wife."

Applause rang out across the room.

Fela took her arm and waked her toward the gate to board their plane.

"You ready, Swan? It's time for us to glide our way across the lake to that place we'll call home."

"Fela, you're getting deep on me again…."

SAVANNAH JENKINS

Fluid Wisdom
A woman's fantasies are her medicine. The stuff her creative,
spiritual and prowess is made of. A man has the same energy
but in a different way. It is important to indulge in the art of
fantasizing fully, without shame, judgment or restraint.

Bound-Savannah Jenkins

"Ready or not here I come," Zane yelled from the bathroom.

I was blindfolded, shackled to a Redwood Southern Canopy bedpost, ready for the unknown. It wasn't easy but I tried to keep my excitement at bay. Didn't want her to see how incredibly excited I was.

Zane had my ankles and wrists tied with black leather straps. My legs wide open. A red silk scarf was around my mouth preventing me from speaking.

I could hear her moving around the room. Then I felt her near me. The heat from her soft skin was hot, like a cup of strong black coffee.

She teased me, lightly brushed up and down my body with a feather. I lay back, took in the sensual scent of a strawberry candle swimming through the air. The smell put my thoughts and body into a meditative trance.

My soul brightened as Zane played with my nipples. She tickled and teased them like she was picking dewberries from a bush. She stayed there for a while...

My body quivered as she put her tongue to my dark, perfectly round nipples. She planted her hot mouth on me like it had gotten stuck on hot ice. I moaned a little, arched my back in an effort to put more of me in her mouth. When she noticed me squirming she removed the scarf from my mouth and shoved in her own beautiful 38DD's.

Not wanting her to think I couldn't handle it, I proceeded to lick her 38's like an ice cream cone. I followed that by sucking them like a vanilla shake through a straw.

I sucked them hard enough to make her let out a loud moan. She slipped her fingers in and out of my mouth and let me lick them. She made her way down my body toward my purring pussy with her other hand. She teased my swollen lips until I was moaning.

Zane loved hearing me call her name so she asked me to say it three times before she continued. If I refused, she promised to spank me and make me stay tied up for hours.

I screamed out in desperate need, "Zane! Zane! Zane! Come on baby, please!"

She slid on top of me and smashed her hot, wet, lightly-furred pussy up against my swollen, well-trimmed, pink-curly kitty cat.

Her grinding up against me like that made me want to cum right then. She rubbed up and down my leg until she couldn't take it anymore.

Her hard, wet clit felt like a Taser poking through a soft suede curtain. She whispered sweet nothings in my ear, asked me quietly to open my hand. When I did she put her wet black cock in my palm. I grabbed it. Begged her to remove my blindfold and let me see her put it in my mouth. She snatched it away and put it up against my pouting lips. Slowly she teased me with it. I opened my mouth wide and waited for her to stick it in. I sucked on it hard. She slid it in deeper and deeper. I continued to suck it and tease her as she watched me.

"Fuck me now. Fuck me now." I begged.

She pulled it away from my mouth and removed my blindfold. She grabbed my hips, lifted my ass and put my pussy up to her mouth. She went at it like it was her last meal.

"Oh my God. Yes. Fuck yes!!" I screamed while she ate it up.

She ate me like fast food, filling her mouth with as much as she could. Sucking, savoring, tasting, nibbling, licking and swallowing up all the juices.

232

I moaned and yelled, "Zane, don't stop. Make me come, baby. Don't stop."

I was at the peak of no return. One false move could cause me to collapse. The louder I screamed the better she performed her one woman show. She started slapping my ass. Spreading my cheeks wide enough for her to stick her big cock in for the grand finale.

With her bionic women powers she fucked me and played with my clit at the same time from the back.

Grabbing my ass and spreading my cheeks was such a turn on for me. I couldn't control it any longer—I came all over her cock. She pushed it in deeper. I convulsed with orgasms and so did she.

The harness rubbing up against her clit sent her to her knees. She looked up at me like she had just finished a marathon. That was when I realized, we were bound....

233

Fluid Wisdom
The act of surrender is the ultimate show of love and intimacy.
Allowing a lover to have complete control, even for a short
while, indicates trust on a level few are willing to risk.
Surrender is an act of love that should be reserved for only
those we feel inherently safe with and of course, completely
enamored by...

Enslaved-Savannah Jenkins

I couldn't stop watching him.

Every night around midnight, Jack would come home from partying. From my bedroom window I would watch him dance, sway back and forth, tipsy as hell from the two-dollar-a-drink happy hour at *Triples*, a bar down the street from where we lived.

A few minutes before the clock struck twelve, I'd starting counting. One, two, three, four, five. By the time I got to five, Jack would walk in the door, drop whatever he was carrying on the floor and start jumping up and down. He'd kick his pants off like he had ants in them. Full of joy, acting like a Amazonian, he'd swing that fat, long cock around like he was playing a game of *Hide Go Get It*.

And just like clockwork, the same sexy, big-tits-and-ass having girls would be hanging on him. Waiting to be copped and felt up by Jack. He stood open and willing as

235

they removed his white button down shirt. He guided them into his so-called love cave.

Janice.

Tracey.

Jayda.

Lauren.

Barely holding themselves up, they would pull, grab and rub on his cock to get that big stick hard. To them, Jack was an ancient find, a masterpiece. He was sexy and definitely qualified for a *Calvin Klein* underwear commercial. Tall, slender, soft black skin, curly black hair with a stomach cut like an antique stainless steel washboard. Gorgeous almond shaped eyes with long, thick lashes. Jack was a real Mandingo but was still gentle and kind to the ladies.

Jack and I worked down the street from each other but had never officially met. We had a few mutual acquaintances in the business world and I knew they'd probably mentioned me in the context of my professional life. But he had no idea what I knew about him. Insane as it was, to me we were inseparable. I viewed what we had as a real relationship. I felt this way because I knew things about him and had done things with him that he could never imagine.

That big package of his caused me to have night sweats. I thought often about it being inside of my mailbox. I knew I would have to shove it in to make it fit. Jack could surely qualify for the book of world records. His cock had to be fourteen, maybe even sixteen inches. I couldn't be sure of the length of it but it was clear and evident that Jack was a ladies man. Every woman he came in contact with would literally throw themselves at his feet and do whatever at the drop of a dime.

While Jack acted like he had no knowledge of my coveting his million dollar prize, I was pretty sure he knew I wanted to cash in on it.

He would leave his curtains and windows wide open allowing me to witness his sexual escapades. Our bedrooms were right next to each other on the fifth floor. I mean we could literally climb in and out of each other's windows.

Tonight felt different. There was something spectacular in the air. When I got home from doing my errands I removed my clothes, slipped on a purple silk robe, grabbed a glass of wine and stood next to my rhinestone-covered vanity, the usual place where I watched Jack do his thing.

I peered into Jack's window and there he was flat on his back by himself. He was naked, watching porn, slowly massaging his hand up and down on his huge cock. Something made him look toward my window. I jumped back to keep him from seeing me.

Tonight he was alone and handling his own business. I watched him as he stroked his shaft with one hand and used the other to lubricate it with lotion. The lotion was dripping and melting down the sides. It looked like thick icing on a cake.

It was hot as hell and this was the best 3D action movie I had ever seen. Jack turned the TV up louder so I could hear the moans of the freaks fucking on the screen. He started rubbing up and down faster, joining his fingers to get a better grip. The faster he rubbed, the wetter I got. I stood in the window watching and getting more turned on by the minute.

He gripped it tighter. His motions reminded me of someone trying to tame an alligator. I watched his upper body jolt upward while his hands tried to choke it. His tight abs flexed making the whole scene look even hotter.

My pussy started to scream for pleasure. I wanted to feel his cock smashing against my ass. I wanted to feel his intense explosion. Every one of his motions was in sync. The rhythm was up and down, up and down. It turned me on more and more.

239

I fiercely played with myself, my intensity matching his stroke by stroke. I let off loud moan seconds later and let the cum drench my fingers. He lifted himself high off the bed as he reached his peak and shot his cum all over his bed. He fell back, looked over at me and smiled. I jumped back in shock. I couldn't believe it. Could it be that he had known I was there all along?

I couldn't move because if I did he would definitely see me. So I stayed right there and within ten minutes the girls were knocking on his door.

Jack jumped up and threw the sheet off his bed. He grabbed a towel and quickly cleaned himself up.

He opened the door and let in the neighborhood's finest. Janice, Lauren, Jayda and Tracey. They were giggling and pulling on Jack. Janice jumped right in the bed, tore off her dress and put her bare ass in the air. She was wet and ready like she always was.

Jack always fucked Janice first. While he fucked her, Tracey kissed and licked Janice's ass. Tracey asked Jack to help her get her pants off. He obliged. While Jack slid her pants down, Jayda and Lauren started giving him a blow job. As they sucked him, he kissed all over Tracey's big round fake tits. He also fingered her, got her super wet and excited.

It was about to be another long exciting night.

I was ready to get my freak on all by myself. I fantasized myself right there in the bed with Jack and the girls. I imagined them sucking and licking all over my body. I could feel Jack beating my pussy so good with that big hard joy stick. Tracey was sexy as hell. She had a nice round ass and juicy tits. I imagined her licking my clit while Jack fucked me. Janice and Lauren were pretty wild too. In my mind I had them slapping my ass while I sucked Tracey's pussy and she sucked on me.

Last but not least, I brought Jayda into my fantasy. I would gladly suck her pussy and have her come in my mouth

241

over and over again. She was gorgeous—tall, had skin the color of molasses. She had full lips and her eyes were mysterious and bold. She had long, brown locks that cascaded down to the small of her back like an African princess. I would make her belong to me and I would be pleased with the fluid of her soul....

Fluid Wisdom
*Our desires are the essence of our being. There is no shame in
wanting what we want. Do harm to none but always seek,
find and have the pleasure your soul requires....*

Reminisce-Savannah Jenkins

Remembering a warrior from my dreams....

It makes me wet all over again. Thinking about his nine-inch sword, a six-pack as solid and dark as night. His frame strong like a powerful Mandingo statue. His hands— hands that were made for building pyramids....

The dream takes place in medieval times. I was the feast fit for a king. I arrived with a shiny golden crown, my white chocolate dessert melted over a fruit-of-the-spring harvest and a sweet crème de' sole.

He was hungry, tired and dying of thirst. I could not wait to feed him. I anticipated being captured. I craved his commands and wanted to fulfill every one of his demands.

His dark eyes pierced me—I was instantly hypnotized by his charm. He told me to spread my legs and lay on the table he sat in front of, that he was ready to devour his hearty buffet. Instead, I fell to his feet, waited for him to lift me up and place me where he wanted.

I could feel his nine-inch sword stabbing me in the leg. It stood at attention, peeking through his brown leather kilt, welcoming me to the feast.

He removed his armor and growled at me. My body quivered at the sound of his voice. I moaned softly and looked him dead in the eyes. He lifted my white peasant dress, snatched it over to the side and took off my panties with his teeth. He grabbed my ass with his big rough hands.

Lavishly, he kissed and licked up and down my ass like he was licking barbeque sauce off a bone. I was soaking wet in a matter of seconds. He lifted my body and tore the rest of the dress right off me.

My breath got heavy. I inhaled and exhaled my raw desire.

I faintly heard the words, "Go ahead and serve yourself. I got you." I did exactly what he told me.

I was not intimidated by his animalistic behavior. I wanted him to unleash his build up all over me. He picked me up and wrapped my legs around his waist. While he held me in the air, he let the tip of his massive gun play inside the outer folds of my grand entrance. My pussy spit a little as he made his entrance then my walls opened up wide and started clapping and yelling out his name.

"Come on in, Hercules. Come on in deeper and deeper. Yes, there you go."

When he reached the top of my pussy he twirled his gun around and around making just enough room for his liquid injection.

He slid it in and out at an incredible pace. I yelled and held on tight for fear of him losing control. He switched up and pushed it in and out slowly. He acted like he was going to take it out but he just wanted to watch it moving in and out of me. I could tell he was really getting turned on by the sound and look of it coming in dry and going out wet.

I was losing control more every minute. He got as wild as an alley cat. His strokes got harder and harder. He held me around the waist and went deeper and deeper.

He got so into it that he flipped me over and entered from the back. I groaned and moaned with pleasure while he pulled my hair, reached around with his strong butterfly fingers and played with my hard clit.

"Harder! Harder! I'm coming." I told him.

He got even more intense. He lifted me up while holding my waist and pounded me until he lost it.

He was slow coming down. Like removing air from a balloon he deflated, slid himself from inside my walls and released a warm fluid down my back. When it was over, he

247

rested on top of me, breathless and hung over. He mumbled the words *thank you.*

I would never forget the dream about my Mandingo warrior....nor would I forget the moment that we became fluid...

Fluid Wisdom
Liberation is the act of living, thinking and being free to love, experience and know your body in the deepest ways possible. Without physical and sexual liberation, freedom is just an idea.

Freedom by Savannah Jenkins

This Yoni will amaze you. She has the power to make any man or woman fall to their feet with a proposal. So sweet and yummy. Has the nerve to be bossy. Her walls flutter throughout the day. She giggles quietly during the night. She is often in heat and lays around in the dark with her doors wide open. She mixes and spins her tangerine mango organic juices. Releases them into the air while sniffing for her prey.

If anyone dares to come near her underground railroad, she'll quiver, throb a little and shut her doors quickly. As she peeks out she looks for fingerprints and listens for footsteps. If she likes your scent she will stand tall and firmly mount herself. Then like a master looking for a runaway she will snatch you, tax you, trap you and wrap her legs around your face, smash your lips onto her walls.

You'll knock and knock trying to escape, afraid of the motion but interested in your position. She pulls you in deeper and deeper. Something about her sweet trail of ecstasy makes you feel alive. If you get the chance to see what freedom feels like and you want her to help you get to the other side.

She likes to play hide and seek. Make you search, try to follow her everywhere she goes. Her wish is your command. You will want to reach that peak of satisfaction. Feeling like you're dying of thirst from the maze she puts you through, you beg harder and louder. She laughs and plays with your head and spits out just a little of her sweetness. You swallow to keep from chocking. Then she spits out a little more.

She is so sweet and refreshing that after tasting her you'll feel revitalized. Comfortable enough to inhale and exhale—you just want to lay there and marinade in freedom.

When you feel you've finally made it, she starts to disappear in the night.

You yell, "Come back! Come back!," and start to gasp for air. Then you realize it was only a wet dream. But go ahead and dream—you now have the freedom....

Fluid Wisdom
Its takes courage to fly. To pack up our dreams and fantasies and soar. To let life and desire guide us. To be free to live as our souls move us. To honor humanity while celebrating ourselves...

Flight #69-By Savannah Jenkins

It was the summer, those months when Palm Springs heat soared to a scorching 113 degrees. I had booked a room at the Riviera—my fav nesting spot in that inner city desert. I was sitting and sipping on my favorite Lemon Drop cocktail. I was topless, laying across a pink Tinker Bell beach towel, listening to music on my Ipod, feeling empowered and uninhibited. I loved the looks of admiration for my firm, perky tits that looked like juicy pomegranates with just a hint of mature Mother Nature.

I stuck my feet in the pool and swished them around in the warm blue water. My motions created baby tsunamis. I sung to myself and watched other sweet female fruit sashay across the pavement. Some trotted around without tops or bottoms—drunken bottomless beauties.

Back in my own world I laid back and closed my eyes for a few. A sexy hot butch came over and tapped me on my shoulder. She kneeled down and asked if I wanted another Lemon Drop or perhaps a hot Latin lover?

I opened my big brown eyes, smiled at her vindictively and said "No thank you, sweetheart."

She smiled—showed me her beautiful, straight, white teeth. I was really feeling her Latin swag. Something about her boyish body language turned me on.

She got me thinking about the time I went out with this sexy, Latin tomboy named LJ. She was fine as hell and oozed sexuality.

Long black hair, dark almond-shaped eyes and skin as soft and pale as a beautiful porcelain doll. LJ always aimed to please. I stayed turned on and ready every time we were together.

My new Latin Diva turned out to be a true gentlewoman. One evening she said she needed to stop by her house before she dropped me off. Those words were like the sound of a Spanish guitar to my ears. The minute she opened her apartment door, I went straight to her bedroom. I removed my panties and stuck them underneath her pillow. I wanted her to wake up to the sweet smell of pussydew, beef bacon and maple syrup.

She came in the bedroom seconds later and asked me what I wanted to do next. I lifted my red rhinestone stiletto and placed it on her leopard print ottoman. I moved my leg open with my hand. Made sure she got a magnified view of my shaved naked pearl.

I had been fantasizing about her blowing me way too long. I decided this would be the night. I stood there open and licking on one of my fingers. My expression told her to come and get it. I made sure she could see my wet lips glazed like a sweet honey bun. I knew she would want to eat it, because she kept a sweet tooth. She watched me for a while then started to lick her lips.

A bright light appeared as she stepped to me like lighting. She kissed me long and passionately, her silky wet

tongue licked up and down my neck leaving a salt trail like a
snail. I was sweet and sour--she was hot and spicy.

I was so ready I grabbed her hand and put it on my
pussywillow. Planted her fingers deep within my wet slippery
walls. I smashed them deeper and deeper. I moaned and so
did she. I felt a trip to Spain coming and positioned myself
for the ride. She dropped down to her knees, looked up at
me with those big pretty eyes and melted my heart. First she
sucked on her fingers then started to blow me slowly.

She nibbled on my lips, licked on my juicy clit and slid
her fingers in and out.

One finger. Yes.

Two fingers. Oh yes.

Three fingers. Yes, oh yes!

She sucked on my clit and reached her fingers up to
my mouth so that I could taste my own sweet juices. It was
intoxicating. I relished in the sexy, beautiful sounds of heavy
breathing and moaning. She whispered to me that she could

imagine my juicy lips on her wet Latin pussy as she put her now sweet tasting fingers on my warm textured tongue.

She played with my apple bottom. Slapped, licked and bit it softly. I welcomed her every move. She took control of my plane—stayed far away from turbulence. The ride was smooth. Before we landed she made a loud announcement.

"Good evening, passengers. There will be a bit of delay. We are being asked to circle around until further notice due to other airlines arriving at the same time. Please continue to keep your seat belts on. We will wait for a ramp to become available."

While the other passengers waited for a ramp to open up, she took me to that special place where everything became fluid again and again until we landed together....

About the Authors

Ifalade Ta'Shia Asanti (Tiffany Maxwell) is an award-winning fiction writer, journalist, filmmaker, poet and television personality. Ta'Shia's essays, short stories and editorials have appeared in distinguished magazines, books and anthologies including *Essence Magazine, Poets & Writers* and many others. TaShia is the author of four books (*The Sacred Door, The Master Breakthrough, The Seer and The Bones Do Talk*). She is also the recipient of the *Kathleen E. Morris Award for Best Contemporary Fiction* and was awarded the *Seed Scholarship Award from the International Black Writers and Artists Organization.* In 2011, TaShia was named a *Fellow* by the *Lambda Literary Foundation* and presented with a scholarship to attend their distinguished UCLA Writer's Program.

Adeloni Dewberry (Savannah Jenkins), breaks literary ground with her sexy stories in this book. Founder of the nationally acclaimed, *Lip Service Spoken Word Show,* her achievements in the business and entertainment world are vast and internationally celebrated. From brokering a landmark distribution deal with *Walgreen's* to carry her original products to launching her own line of urban fashion, as well as an original line of beauty and wellness products. Over the years, *Adeloni* has dressed mega stars in film and TV.

For more information about book signings and readings by the authors, go to www.tiffanyandsavannah.com